'It's the Lord's doing and it is marvelous in our eyes! Indeed, it is victory at last. The storm is over, glory to Jesus. The University of Nigeria, Nsukka, I am here for you. A lioness is here, so make way everyone. Father Lord, I do not take this for granted, thank you. This can only be you. I nearly gave up on my dream of becoming a mass communicator. I paid heavily three times to gain admission into the University of Nigeria, Nsukka, but all my efforts were totally in vain. This is my fourth attempt. I asked God to intervene, and He did. I didn't pay anyone; I only studied as if my whole life depended on studying. I'm excited that my dream has come true. This is nothing but a stepping stone to my bright future.' Chioma soliloquized while dancing around her room joyfully.

Chioma was the only daughter of Mr & Mrs Stephen Okeke. She had previously written JAMB four times but kept scoring below the cut-off mark. However, her last attempt was a huge surprise to everyone who knew how hard she had struggled to pass or at least reach the University cut-off mark. In her last attempt, she scored 300 in Jamb and 295 in the University's POST UTME (Unified Tertiary Matriculation Examination). While preparing for the exams, she denied herself so many pleasures like watching movies, constant stay on social media, night sleep and procrastination. She prepared for her JAMB and POST UTME as if her life depended on it.

Chioma's parents were in their sitting room that faithful evening, relaxing and watching a program on the television when Chioma broke the good news of her long-awaited admission into UNN, one of the best universities in Nigeria, to study Mass Communication. Chioma's mother unconsciously burst into songs of joy.

'Oh I could sing endless songs

Of how you saved me from shame

And I could dance a thousand miles

Because of Your great love and faithfulness.

My heart is exploding Lord

To tell of all You've done:

Of how you took away my humiliation

And wiped away the shame of my past.

I wanna scream it out!

From every rooftop praise God....'

'Yes, ooo! Papa Chioma, didn't I tell you that my daughter is not a nonentity? My Chioma has proved to everybody that she is not a dimwit.' Mrs Okeke enunciated excitedly. She kept singing, dancing, talking, and jumping around throughout that evening. It was a dream comes true for her.

'Mama Chioma, I never called my daughter a nonentity or a dimwit. Chioma is a child of destiny and a prophecy waiting to be fulfilled. Have you forgotten what the big man of God who came to our church for the annual convention told you when Chioma was still in your womb? Big daddy said that Chioma was a daughter of conciliation, a voice that her generation and generations after her won't forget. He also said that she was a star that would stand out and shine brighter and brighter,' Mr Okeke said defensively.

'Mama Chioma, you know I'm still expecting my salary, unlike you who doesn't need a salary. Please, you will pay our daughter's acceptance fee and school fee, when my salary comes, I will complete the remaining payment,' Mr Okeke said excitedly.

'You know that there won't be a problem between us. We always quarrel over the issue of money, and the most annoying part of it is that, sometimes, you would promise to pay me back, but unfortunately, all I would get in the end is a failed promise. However, as far as my only daughter is concerned, I will do everything possible to support her,' Mrs Okeke snapped without looking at her husband.

Mrs Okeke was a big-time businesswoman. She had a supermarket where she sold mainly provisions and food items, while her husband was a civil servant. Mr Okeke, whose salary was often delayed, saw financial responsibility in the house as something that had to be shared between him and his wife, but his wife always fought against that ideology. Mrs Okeke thought that her husband as the head of the family should be able to head the family financially. Mr & Mrs Okeke also had another son after giving birth to Chioma. They had waited on God for six years before having him. They had only two children who were Chioma and Obinna; they cared and supported their children in every area.

'Dad and Mum, you both should not start with your cat and dog attitude now. Besides, the school portal is not yet open for any payment.' Chioma glowed.

'But who told you the school portal was not open for any payment? You know I don't like late payment for any reason. It is always good to avoid late payment to prevent telling stories that touch the heart.' Mrs Okeke advised.

'Mum, Mercy, that my friend who gained admission last year, told me that. She was even the one who sent me the admission list. According to her, the school portal will likely open in the next two weeks for payment,' she responded to her Mum excitedly.

From the onset, Mrs Okeke had always paid her children's school fees on time. When it was her husband's turn to pay, she made sure she persuaded him to bring the money on time. The reason behind her eagerness to pay fees on time was the fear that had been installed in her when she missed her common entrance exam because of late payment. She then vowed to herself never to pay any fee late.

'Where is Obinna?' Mr Okeke asked no one in particular.

Both the daughter and the mother kept quiet. They knew how angry he would be to know that his only begotten son was still in someone's house at that time of the day. One of Mr Okeke's policies was that no one was permitted to be in someone's house once it was 6:00 pm. Chioma wanted to leave the sitting room to prevent lying to her father because she and her brother were taught never to lie for any reason, and she was afraid of what would happen to her brother if she told their father the truth. As she tried to elude, her father called her back and insisted she tell him where her brother went to.

'Dad, I think he went to see one of his friends. He is on his way back home,' she said, trembling.

'I see. So that was what you people were hiding? You see, I won't spare your son today. How can a responsible child be in a friend's house by 7:00 pm? Both he and his friend are irresponsible. If your friend is not responsible enough to know that his time in your house has expired, then you as a responsible person should be able to tell him to go. Children of this generation are something else. I will deal with this boy when he comes back. Since he has refused to learn, he has to learn the hard way. In as much as he is still under my care, he won't have his way. Not in this house,' Mr Okeke yelled.

Both mother and daughter tried to calm him down, but the more they tried, the angrier he became. After much pleading from his wife, he forgave his son for the last time.

Mr Okeke was a disciplinarian who made sure he never spared any of his children when they committed unpardonable offences like; lying, stealing, staying out late, and so on. He indeed provided anything they needed, but he was a man who could not accept any excuse for a mistake made. He was a tyrannical and short-tempered father but a calm husband. He tolerated every wrong decision his wife made patiently but had zero tolerance for his children's mistakes. At the earlier years of their marriage, Mr Okeke was not a calmed husband. He was always picking out his wife's faults. Naturally, he was a short tempered man. His wife always repealed against him and his decisions which often led to heated arguments. Mr Okeke advised himself and took the decision to selflessly live in peace with his wife the day he lost his temper and slapped his wife. That was the only day he raised his hand on his wife and he hated himself for making that mistake. He was from a family where their father always beat their mother at any slightest provocation. After witnessing how their mother always cry after been beaten by their father, he vowed never to treat his wife the way their father treated their mother.

'Chioma, I thank God your father has let your brother off, but I will give that boy a serious warning he will not be able to forget in a hurry.' Mrs Okeke voiced out.

'Please bring out a small bowl of soup from the freezer for me and your dad. You and your brother should eat the remaining yam and sauce, Ada. Don't forget to tell your brother not to kill the turkey again so that it will be used for Church Thanksgiving tomorrow,' Mrs Okeke further instructed Chioma.

***** ***** *****

'Praise the Lord!' Mummy Elele the Pastor's wife shouted.

'Hallelujah!' The congregation thundered.

'I intentionally told Chioma to stand aside so that she would be the last testifier,' Mummy Elele uttered. This made the congregation start making a joyful noise to the Lord, and clapping their hands.

Chioma was a church worker; not just a church worker, but a very good girl. Almost every mother in the church wanted their girl child to be like Chioma. Another thing that made Chioma attractive was her humility. She was down to earth. Nearly all the single brothers in her church queued up to say hi to her after every Sunday service and Thursday fellowship.

Chioma was a very beautiful girl with a nice body shape. She was a tall and curvy girl. No man in his right sense would pass her without turning to behold the beauty queen with dark skin colour. Some people said she took her father's complexion while others said she took her mother's body structure. Her beauty intimidated some sisters in the church, and it attracted jealousy and hatred towards her.

'Praise the Lord!' Chioma shouted.

'Hallelujah!' The congregation thundered.

'I want to testify to the glory of God. His mercy is ever with me. Indeed, God is my faithful father whose constant love is better than life itself. He has done what no man can do. He has fulfilled His promise in my life. At a point, I gave up on gaining admission to study Mass Communication at the University of Nigeria, Nsukka, but the Lord surprised me when I almost gave up the dream. Today, I stand before you to testify that the Lord has granted my heart desire.' Chioma testified.

The congregation could not contain their joy at that point. Everybody began to shout and clap for the Lord.

Chioma shouted 'amen' in the microphone which made the Church quiet again.

Chioma continued. 'I want to use this opportunity to encourage anyone who is passing through one challenge or the other not to give up on God. Has God promised you anything? Believe Him, for those who trust in Him, can never be confounded. Believe and trust your God who knows the number of hairs on your head. Trust and obey any instruction He has given you for there's no other way to be happy but to trust and obey. I pray God will grant me the grace to remain faithful to Him, not to be influenced negatively on the campus. People will see me and see Jesus.'

The congregation shouted 'amen' as Chioma dropped the microphone and stood aside.

'O Lord, my God, when I in awesome wonder

Consider all the worlds Thy Hands have made

I see the stars, I hear the rolling thunder

Thy power throughout the universe displayed....'

While the choristers were still singing Carl Gustav Boberg's hymns, Chioma's parents, brother, friends, and well-wishers brought an offering and thanksgiving items to the altar. After the pastor's wife prayed for Chioma, they all retired to their various seats.

TWO

The University of Nigeria, Nsukka, had limited hostels for her students. Most students desired to stay in the school hostels because of the constant light in the school, available wifi, free water supply, tight security, and so on. UNN had seven luxurious females and three male hostels. Each student's hostel accommodation was meant to expire after an academic session. This gave some other unfortunate female students, especially those who were unlucky to get hostel accommodation, an opportunity to pay their school fees on time and stand the chance of getting accommodation. However, some students who were lucky to get accommodation in the previous academic session might not be lucky enough to get it in the next academic session.

Some students who depended wholly on the hostel accommodation ended up frustrated when disappointed. While some students resorted to lodges because of hostel frustration, other lucky ones found people who were able to squat them either for free or with payment. The struggle for hostel accommodation had been a tussle for UNN students, especially her female students. There were still some students, especially male students, who preferred a lodge to a hostel because of their privacy and other reasons known to them. Each room in the UNN hostel accommodated four students, especially female hostels, but because of the limited hostels, many rooms usually accommodated more than four students, which resulted in overpopulation in hostels.

Chioma walked tiredly and entered Eyoita, room 103. After she closed the door behind her, her eyes went straight to her six-spring student mattress, and she saw the bed sheet on the floor. Her face became sullen immediately. The small table she was sharing with her second-year roommate was also in a mess and this added to her anger.

Chioma resumed school barely a week ago and she had not familiarized herself with her roommates. Everybody was a stranger to her. Chioma kept on wondering why she would come back every day and see her little corner in a total mess. But for once, she had never seen her final year roommate's corner scattered nor her third-year roommate's corner scattered. She kept on wondering who was scattering everywhere for her whenever she went out. She decided to confront her second-year roommate who was always in the room even when everybody had gone out.

'Promise, what happened to my bed and my table side?' Chioma asked angrily. Promise, her second-year roommate, kept mute. Chioma asked her again out of anger.

'I'm not your corner keeper, am I?' Chioma's question made Promise flare up.

Chioma became afraid because she thought Promise would fight her and beat her up because of how she reacted like a wounded lioness. Chioma started apologizing to her for asking about her corner. Chioma felt it was too early for her to start having a problem with her roommate. 'I'm sorry if I have offended you with my question. It is just that I'm not happy seeing my corner like this whenever I come back from lectures.' Chioma apologized sincerely.

'Chioma, it's okay. I have been having stomach pain for some days now. The pain doesn't even allow me to know what I'm doing. Sorry for scattering your corner for you,' Promise suddenly apologized too.

The room was a four-man room with six-spring single bunk and little space for each student. The first bunk was called corner A, reserved for the final-year student in the room. The second bunk was called corner B, for the third-year student in the room. The third bunk, corner C, was for the second-year student in the room. And the fourth bunk was called corner D, reserved for the first-year student in the room. In most of the female hostels, the first-year student and the third-year student stayed at the right-hand side of the room while the second-year student and the final year student stayed at the left-hand side of the room. Each room had three medium-sized wooden tables at the centre of the room, separating the right-hand side of the room from the left-hand side of the room.

Promise was groaning in pain when Divine entered the room followed by Chinwe. Divine was the third-year student in the room. She was the 'book warm type'; from the lecture class to the library, then to church and the night class. Divine was good at combining her studies and her religious life; none of them lagged. She was the quietest in the room.

Chinwe was the final-year student in the room who believed in doing the right thing at the right time. Chinwe was the type of student who could never trade her academic life or her social life for any reason. On some weekends, Chinwe would follow some of her friends to attend a nightclub. According to her, it was a way of cooling the brain.

For Promise, she was a complacent student. She believed that one did not need to overstress herself in school to pass an exam. Promise's favourite quote was, 'I can't kill myself and die, and UNN will still be in existence.' That was why she failed two of her departmental courses in her first year. When the first semester result came out and she saw that she failed two courses, she foolishly went to the two lecturers in charge of the courses respectively to offer her body in exchange of some marks that would at least make her not to carry those courses over. Unfortunately, those lecturers slept with her three times without adding any mark for her.

Promise kept groaning in pain, which made her roommates start panicking. They wanted to take her to the school clinic but she refused, insisting she would be alright. Divine brought a pain relief tablet and wanted to force Promise to drink it but Chinwe stopped her from forcing Promise to take the drug.

'Divine, do not coerce her to take this drug, it will only worsen her pains. I think I know what is wrong with her. She is not having a menstrual cramp,' Chinwe told Divine.

Divine and Chioma started asking Chinwe what was wrong with Promise but she refused to let them know anything. She told them that Promise would be fine in a few days and that it was a minor issue.

Promise had taken an abortion pill last three days ago and it was separating her intestines inside her. Yet, even though she had been in great pains for two days now, her attitude showed she was not frightened. She knew she would be back to her feet after four days of torture.

It was not her first time aborting a pregnancy. She was influenced in her first year by her final-year roommate who had handed her over to her course mate. Promise started dating the guy and packed a few of her things to the guy's lodge. The guy's lodge mates saw Promise as their wife because they lived as a couple. Promise was a faithful school wife to her boyfriend because she never looked at any other guy's face except when she slept with two of her departmental lecturers for mark. Lately, she had started considering breaking up with the guy because each time she became pregnant; the guy would buy an abortion pill for her and take her back to the hostel to suffer alone. This was the sixth time it was happening. She had told her boyfriend about it, but the guy told her that he did not want his lodge mates to know she was pregnant or that she was aborting the pregnancy to avoid gossip.

'Promise, I must tell you the truth, you have to be very careful if you still want to live long,' Chinwe told Promise who was lying on the floor.

Divine and Chioma were still in the dark; they were wondering why Promise had to be careful in order not to die untimely. Chinwe had aborted once, so she understood what Promise was passing through. She had gone for night class one fateful day. Along the line, she became tired of reading, so she decided to pay her boyfriend whose lodge was not very far from where she was reading a surprise night visit, but it was unfortunate for her. On her way, she was stopped by two cultists and was raped. She became pregnant and started avoiding her boyfriend. When she was pregnant for two months, Wendy, her close friend noticed it, which made her open up to her friend. Wendy took her to where she bought an abortion pill. She passed through hell; in fact, she thought she would never survive it. After that experience, she hated anything called night class.

'Roomies, please, I want to collect something from my course mate upstairs and I will not go with my phone because I want it to charge. My friend Wendy is already on her way; please tell her to wait patiently for me when she comes,' Chinwe announced, intending to break the uncomfortable silence in the room. She continued, 'Before I forget, there will be a night show at the Old Carolina hotel this night, and you don't need to worry about transportation because there will be a free bus at freedom square by 8 pm and your security is assured. Trust me, this night will be fun and the gate fee is free for ladies. Just come if you want to see the most famous Nigerian artists live and direct. You will never regret it.'

Divine's facial expression showed that she was surprised by what Chinwe said. She couldn't figure why Chinwe would be planning to attend the night party when her roommate was in great pain.

'Chinwe, you perplex me. You are talking about a party when your roommate is passing through hell experience. Aside from that, it is barely a week since school resumed and you have started attending parties,' Divine told Chinwe calmly.

'See kettle calling pot black. Haven't you started night class, and it is barely one week since school resumed? My department, Chemistry, does not give me any breathing space, so I need to enjoy this weekend while it lasts because I don't know when I will be free again to attend a party. I have told you that Promise will be fine in no time.' Chinwe chuckled.

Chinwe turned to Chioma who was on her bed observing everything that was going on in the room, 'Chioma, dear, you are welcome once again to the den where lions and lionesses fight without fainting. No one is looking at your face, so don't be deceived, you have to fight your way out. This is my final year at UNN, and I must admit that UNN is not like some other universities where students play around and do well when the semester result comes out. I'm not saying that one will now kill herself with books. To me, one has to read but still create little time to have fun and ease off the UNN stress. That is the reason I made sure I attended some parties when I had the chance to do so.'

Divine did not hide her opposition to what Chinwe just said. 'See, Chioma, there are still other ways to ease off stress aside from being present in all the parties in and outside UNN. You can join a Bible-believing church or fellowship. Staying amidst brethren revives one's soul, spirit, and mind. You can also take your time and rest after lectures and personal study,' Divine said in self-defence she turned to Promise who was now calm to ask for her opinion on the topic.

'You guys should leave my school daughter alone. She is on her mother's side. I need to warn my daughter seriously so she doesn't endanger her life in UNN,' Chinwe said quickly, saving Promise the stress of talking.

All the roommates started laughing. The room was becoming lively for Chioma who initially thought that the room would be boring for her. She was amazed by the level of their cooperation. They were behaving like sisters, though they had their unique positive and negative characters respectively.

When the room was becoming quiet again, Chinwe cleared her throat which drew all attention to her bed where she was seated. 'I have almost forgotten that I want to go upstairs and rent an outfit I will wear tonight for the party from one of my course mates. Yet before I go, I would like to share my testimony with you guys.' Chinwe pronounced cheerfully, and this made her roommates wonder.

Chinwe continued when she saw that she had their undivided attention. 'I got a job as a salesgirl somewhere in Lagos. Initially, my uncle whom I was staying with refused me from doing any work; he only wanted me to stay indoors and rest, but I couldn't imagine myself staying in the house for about three months. Before school vacated, it had always been my dream to spend my long vacation in Lagos. I dreamt of finding a decent job there and having some personal savings.

So, one fateful morning, I left my uncle's house around 5 am to avoid the terrible holdup one meets at Oshodi, Lagos on Mondays. I wanted to be at the shop before 7 am to please my boss. For about two weeks after I started work, my boss had been complaining about my lateness to work, but it was not my fault because my uncle's house was far from my workplace. As I was trekking to a nearby bus stop to board a bus, I heard a man's voice commanding me to halt. The only words that came to my mind then were: this is Lagos, shine your eyes. I doubled my pace, but the same voice commanded me again, that was when I knew that the person was very close to me, so I stopped.

When I turned to see who had the impetus to command me that early morning, I saw four men following me. Two of the men were already very close to me. I became afraid. Running was not an option for me because they were very close to me; neither was shouting an alternative because we were the only ones on the road at that particular time. I was sure that fighting them would be suicidal because those men were young and healthy.

When I was still thinking about what I would do, one of them commanded me to give them my handbag. I wanted to plead with them when one of them immediately raised his shirt to show me the pistol he hid in his front trouser pocket. Much fear gripped me, so without wasting time, I gave them the new handbag my guy bought for me before I left Nsukka. Before I could open my mouth to ask them whether or not I should go, I saw two men in police uniforms approaching where we were. I didn't even know when I started shouting for help; this made those police walk faster to us. I thought those men would have run when they saw the police, but to my greatest surprise, they didn't. I didn't wait for the police to ask me what the problem was; I began to shout that those men were criminals.

Without hesitation, the police handcuffed the four men, and they still didn't react. One of the policemen told me that we would all be going to the police station so that I would testify against those men, and I naively agreed. Before I knew what was happening, we had already walked for about twenty minutes in the bush. I began to ask myself whether or not the police station was located inside the bush. One of the police called me back to reality when he shouted at me to walk faster. In a short while, we arrived at a wild field that looked like a deserted village square with uncompleted building. My fear knew no bounds at this point. I felt I had reached a destination of no return. All the men, including the policemen, sat on some wooden, old chairs that were there; I was the only one standing. They were busy smiling at one another; I lost the courage to ask them where I was.

After summoning courage, I decided to ask those policemen whether or not the place they were talking about was the police station. As I opened my mouth to talk, one of the police officers motioned everyone to be still and calm. The policeman who had motioned them to be still started addressing them in a language I couldn't comprehend. I paid close attention, wanting to understand what was going on. At a point, all the men busted out in laughter, which made my fear triple because it was obvious they were selling me with an unknown language.

At this point, I needed no prophet to prophesy to me that those men were working together. I can't remember the last time I went on my knees to pray to God. I became a prayer warrior suddenly. Don't criticize me for forgetting the last time I prayed, it wasn't intentionally. Most times, I slept off whenever I wanted to pray or my conscience became clouded with many thoughts. That is not the problem for now, so I began to ask God for mercy and intervention.

One of the men told the officers to remove their handcuffs and handcuff me with one of them; he said that in the English language which was why I understood him. I didn't stop praying in my heart because it was my only hope of survival at that moment. As one of the officers was handcuffing me, one of the men said something that made him turn to me to reply. The man repeated himself as if he wanted to make his point clearer. The few words I understood were I, yesterday, last, today, first, because he mixed the language with English. The next thing I saw was that those men started arguing. I guess they were arguing about who would devour me first before the arrival of their boss. They were so engrossed with their argument that they didn't notice when I started drawing back. I ran as soon as I was out of their sight. Sincerely, I don't know how I left their presence; neither do I know how I found my way back to my uncle's house that day. The only thing I know is that it was the Lord's doing,' Chinwe narrated her story calmly without interruption from any of her roommates.

The atmosphere in the room changed as all of them became emotional. Chioma was on the verge of shedding tears while Promise was already crying as if she had been waiting for that moment to cry out the pain in her heart. Divine was speaking in tongue and praising God for the wonders He had done. After a while, Chinwe left the room without talking to anyone.

THREE

'I don't understand what is happening to everybody around me. It seems as if everyone has gone crazy or I have gone insane.' Chioma was soliloquizing when a lady sitting close to her at the school library touched her to tell her that she was disturbing the peace of other students with her loud thoughts. Chioma apologized to the lady for disturbing other students reading around her with her matter.

Chioma had been in the library for about two hours thinking about the number of guys that had been disturbing her for the past month. She was beginning to have issues with every guy's craving to have her: her lecturers, course mates, and strange guys. Initially, she thought it was normal until she discovered that no day would pass without her having a strange encounter with one guy or another. Some of the guys would politely ask her out which she respectfully declined, while some insisted on her becoming their girlfriend whether she liked it or not.

On the other hand, her mother contributed to issues in her head. It was barely a week but her mum had already given Chioma's phone number to three of her friends' sons, expecting Chioma to choose one from the three who would be her husband. Chioma's mother had the intention of choosing the right husband for her daughter who would take over the responsibility of sponsoring her education. Her parents wanted to concentrate on Chioma's brother. Chioma's mother also believed that girls were like flowers that had their season of flourishing and season of withering. To Chioma's mother, that was Chioma's flourishing season because she was already twenty-three years old.

Last week, Chioma had her worst night class experience at the Faculty of Arts' theatre. A guy came to sit beside her. At first, she kept quiet because she felt there was no other space for the guy to seat except beside her. She soon became uncomfortable when she noticed that the guy was not reading but gawking at her. She ignored the guy and pretended to be reading but she was aware of the number of times the guy blinked. When the guy's presence became unbearable for her, she took her books and went to another chair and sat. The guy still followed her to where she was. Chioma began to wonder whether the guy was insane. It was then that she saw that almost all the students who came for night class were already sleeping. She was not surprised because it was a norm for almost all the students who came to tonight class to be sleeping by that time except a few ones who insisted on not sleeping at all. She was still thinking about what to do besides leaving the hall by that deadly time of the night when the guy cleared his throat. She ignored him and was seriously reading her book but she knew that her mind was not on the book she was reading. This was when he tapped her on the shoulder with a beaming smile.

'Hi, Miss Beauty,' the guy greeted her. It was then that Chioma recognized him as one of the notorious guys in UNN.

'Hello,' Chioma replied him, looking straight into his eyes. The guy coyly turned his face down.

After some seconds of silence between the two, the guy raised his head to face Chioma. 'I don't know if I'm supposed to introduce myself to you but I'm sure that both new and old students in UNN know me. Well, my name is the Boss but my friends call me Viper. I'm a final year student of Political Science,' the guy introduced himself presumptuously.

Chioma had seen the guy, on some occasions, with his gangs vandalizing the school's properties. She had heard so many terrible things about the Boss popularly known as the Viper but she didn't know he was the one because he was not wearing his regular uniform; yellow trouser, red shirt, and blue face cap. Rather he was wearing a white kaftan. The Boss was known for his lack of fear for anyone and good combat skills. Most of the lecturers feared him because he was a dead human being. He masterminded most of the rape cases heard in UNN. One sad thing was that whenever the school authority planned to expel him from school, nobody would see him again for that period. However, many students rumored that the school authority always let him off because his father was one of the top Nigeria politicians. So he always went scot free even after committing tremendous offences.

'Miss Beauty, don't be afraid because I have not come to frighten you. I only came to express my feelings for you. You must be wondering by now how I know you but that is not the issue now. What matters to me is that the most beautiful and outstanding student in UNN did not go unnoticed for the Viper. Seriously, you are the most beautiful and outstanding student on this Campus. For the past one month now, I have been sending my guys to stalk you but you proved to me that you are not just an ordinary girl. You have won my award and you have made me come to you and profess my feelings, what I have never done in UNN. If I want any girl on this campus I send my guys to get the girl for me but your case is different,' the guy continued talking while she was busy checking her time and praying for the time to be 5 am so that she could escape to her hostel.

She knew how brutal the guy could be which was why she patiently waited for the words in his mouth to finish without interrupting him. When Chioma could not take his endless ramblings any longer, she decided to tell the guy that he was disturbing her but she remembered how violent the guy was the last time she saw him and his gangs destroying things, so she kept quiet.

A few weeks ago, she saw the same guy protesting against the prohibition of guys entering female hostels. This same Viper guy was the one exhilarating his gangs that day. Some girls were saying in the hostel that day that those guys protesting were cultists and that was the day she marked his face. On another occasion, Chioma was coming back from the library one day when she saw some students running. She had no idea why those students were running but she also joined them to run for her life. It was when she entered her hostel that she heard some girls saying that those cultists were still protesting against the prohibition of guys entering female hostels.

Chioma became more worried when she saw the guy licking his lips licentiously as he was staring at her breasts. Her fear and worry disappeared when she suddenly started hearing people's 5 am alarms. The alarms woke many students; they began to pack their books to go back to their hostels or lodges. Chioma also put her books and the wrapper she used in covering her legs because of too much of mosquito bites. She happily announced to him that the time was 5 am, and they would have to continue their discussion the next time they met in night class, and she left without waiting for his response. Chioma knew she would never come to tonight class again so she would not see that guy and his likes.

Her thoughts moved to two of her lecturers who threatened to fail her if she refused to comply with them. Dr Udo and Dr Eze were Chioma's lecturers who taught the same course. Just like it was said that two birds fly together, both lecturers were best of friends with the same attitude.

It was last week Monday, after their last class that Chioma's course rep came to her and told her that both lecturers wanted to see her in their office after their last class for the day. Chioma's heart skipped when her course rep told her that. From her first year till this her third year, none of the lecturers had said anything to her except replying her greetings. Rumor had it that those two lecturers had unfinished business with anything on skirts. Chioma was a bit confused on why those lecturers wanted to see her in their office, they shared the same office. She contemplated within her on going to their office with someone but later decided against it. She became more curious to find out why those lecturers wanted to see her so she began to wait for her lectures to end.

Their office door opened when Chioma was about to knock on the door and a female student left the office. She immediately changed her mind on seeing those lecturers, she was about to turn back when Dr Udo saw her and politely called her full name. She respectfully answered and went inside the office and Dr Udo motioned her to close the door behind her. She felt as if she came for a job interview at that time. Dr Eze motioned her to sit on a chair that was opposite his executive chair. There was pin-drop silence in the office; the office became as quiet as a cemetery.

'Sir, my course rep told me you want to see me in your office,' Chioma said to none of them in particular. Chioma became skeptical when Dr Udo left the office and made sure the door was properly closed. She was beginning to suspect the movement in the office.

Dr Eze adjusted his suit and scanned Chioma with his eyes as he wanted to know what was in her mind.

'Chioma dear, I know you are a good girl and one who is determined to accomplish her goals. I have been observing you since your first year and from my findings, you are an extraordinary girl. Whenever I supervise your class during exams, I look for you and monitor you closely but to my greatest surprise, you always mind your papers even when there is an opportunity to cooperate in the exam hall. It did not stop there; your grades are always outstanding.

Lecturers from other departments who handle you on outside courses always come to our department to ask for this smart Mass Communication student. Seriously, if you continue like this, you will likely end up becoming Nsukka's best graduating student (BGS) for next year. You are a true definition of beauty with brain,' He said, adoringly.

All Chioma could say to Dr Eze was thank you because the things he said were no longer new to her. It had always been her goal to become UNN's best graduating student in her set so she took her studies very seriously and God honored her determination to succeed.

Chioma became restless when she saw how Dr Udo looking at her and biting his lips. She asked him for permission to leave but Dr Eze refused. He told her that he had not stated his intention for calling her. He stood up and went to where Chioma was sitting. He drew a side table that was there closer to him and sat on it.

'Dear, I know you may not have noticed that I love you. But I sincerely do. It has always been my dream to have you in my arms but all this while I didn't know how to communicate my feelings to you,' He said passionately and began to caress his lips.

Chioma stood immediately to leave the office but he drew her back and hugged her tightly. It was as if she suddenly started enjoying the whole thing because she kept quiet and relaxed on Dr Eze's shoulder. This sent a go-ahead signal to Dr Eze who took his hand under her top and was stroking her stomach. It was when he wanted to put his hand inside her bra and fondle her breasts that she pushed him forcefully. He nearly landed on the floor because of the hard push.

'I'm not that cheap, sir.' Chioma forced the words out of her mouth. She was very close to the door when Dr Eze ordered her to stop and she obeyed him. He pleaded with her to let them continue with what they had already initiated. He told her that it would be unfair for her to leave him in that condition knowing well that she had aroused him. Chioma controlled her anger in order not to abuse him. She told him to hurry home and meet his wife instead of disgracing himself and his family.

Dr Eze got married to a timid village girl last two years. That was when Chioma was till in her first year. Most girls he promised marriage and slept with felt offended when they heard the sudden news about his marriage. Some of the victimized girls who were courageous enough tried confronting him a few times for explanation but he treated them like fools and threatened to make sure they don't graduate from the university if they failed to stay on their lanes.

Out of fear that Chioma would expose him, he threatened to give her a grade of C in his course. Chioma had made sure she never scored grade C no matter how hard a course maybe. To her, scoring grade C was equivalent to having a grade of F. she detested grade C because she knew the implication of the grade on one's result. Chioma pleaded with Dr Eze not to try anything that would ruin her efforts but he insisted that Chioma allowed him to have access to her body first. It was then that Dr Udo entered the office.

'I can see that all is not going on well here. See, Chioma, this life is very simple and easy but some people have chosen to make things difficult for themselves,' Dr Udo expressed his anger. Dr Udo continued advising Chioma, 'Dear, we all know that you are a bright student but there is what is called mutual benefit. Give us the privilege to be your close friends. I mean allow Dr Eze to be close to you. Trust me you will never regret it. Dr Eze here has everything a woman needs. And don't give me the excuse of him being married because it doesn't matter. As I speak to you now, he will soon divorce that woman because she has never made him happy for once. Almost all the female students in our department want to be close to Dr Eze but his heart beats for you. He is my friend and I'm sure of what I'm saying.'

Dr Udo was another version of Dr Eze, the two met at UNN during their undergraduate days. They had been friends since then though Dr Udo refused to marry because he hated being committed to one person. He was having a good time changing women like he changes cloth.

Chioma was smiling when Dr Udo was talking to her this made them think that she had already fallen for their deceit but her response took them aback.

'I'm not going to give your request a second thought not to talk of doing it. Don't bother about giving me C. You can score me an F; it doesn't mean anything again to me. Sir, before that day comes, let your heart be prepared to answer me wherever you are called. As for evidence against you, it's here on my phone; every aspect of our discussions was recorded.' Chioma did not wait for their response before she hurriedly left the office. She knew that they would come after her to seize her phone so she started running immediately she left their office. When she saw them following her with full speed, she entered the next class through the back door unnoticed and was fortunate to see a female lecturer lecturing her students. Dr Eze and his friend gave up on waiting for her after a while.

Gangangan! Gangangan! The library bell brought Chioma back to reality. When she checked her wristwatch and saw that she had spent about two hours in the library without reading anything, she became angry with herself. She gently packed her books and started heading towards the exit.

'This school is gradually becoming annoying. How can they be locking the library by 7 pm when the school timetable they gave us says that the library opens by 7 am and closes by 10 pm daily except on weekends when it opens by 9 am and closes by 8 pm? It wasn't like this in my first year. Since this man became our new Vice-Chancellor, things have not remained the same. Librarians open and close the library whenever they feel like it. Insecurity has become the order of the day and some lecturers have grown wings. Even non-academic staffs are misbehaving without anyone querying them.' Chioma heard two students who were also leaving the library discussing

FOUR

The recent events happening to Chioma weighed her down completely. She stopped being the lively girl people use to know. Chioma who had formed the habit of smiling and greeting everybody suddenly started being mean to everybody. She became a snub, different from what most of her course mates knew her as when they were in the second semester, first year. Chioma was the type of student who would never raise her hand to answer any question in class except the question was thrown to her directly. Everybody knew she wouldn't raise her hand to answer any question, not because she didn't know the answer, but because she was waiting for the question to be directed to her personally. There was no time she disappointed any lecturer who asked her any question, even the most difficult questions.

However, after the incident that took place between Chioma, Dr Eze, and Dr Udo, she began to isolate herself from others. Everything about her changed except the fact that she still didn't disappoint any lecturer who asked any kind of question. The level of her intellect was amazing to everyone. Most of her course mates' dreams were to be like her but there were some others, especially her female course mates, who hated everything about her because they saw her as their rival. Some of Chioma's acquaintances started showing concern by asking her what the problem was but she didn't open up to any of them. Some others pretended to be concerned, but who only wanted to satisfy their curiosity; they thought she had been raped. The only answer she gave some of her acquaintances who insisted on knowing what was wrong with her was that she had decided to become a lone ranger.

'Bestie, you have been avoiding me for like a week now. In fact, to me, you have avoided me for decades but I won't take it lightly with you again. It's either you tell me what your problem is or I will create a scene here,' Donald said persistently.

The lecture had just ended for the day and Chioma was in a hurry to leave the classroom to prevent anyone from bothering her life with questions. She was about to leave her seat when Donald who always sat beside her in each of their classes blocked her from passing. She tried forcing herself to go through but Donald insisted. He was about to create a scene when Chioma sat down and told him that she would tell him everything.

Both parents of Donald were indigenes of Nsukka. Donald was the only son of his parents, and his father was one of the influential professors in the Religion department. This was why many students who knew him wanted to befriend him. Donald was Chioma's only close, male friend. Both of them became friends in their second semester, first year. That fateful evening, when lectures had ended for the day, Chioma was in a hurry to go to the school library when Donald blocked her way. He offered to accompany her to her hostel but she declined and told him she was not heading to the hostel but the library. He then told her that he was also heading to the school library, and both of them went to the library together. As Donald initiated a conversation on their way to the library, Chioma realized how smart and intelligent Donald was. Hence, both became inseparable friends. Most of their course mates thought both of them were dating. Donald's girlfriend who was also in the same department with them broke up with him when she also found their closeness unbearable. It was after Donald's girlfriend broke up with him that he started developing unusual feelings for Chioma. No day would pass without Donald phoning Chioma to check on her although they both see each other in class. That was also when he started calling her Bestie which means best friend. Initially, Chioma refused answering the name and would always frown whenever

Donald called her Bestie but with time, she unconsciously accepted the name and started answering.

Donald was not just an intelligent fellow but a handsome guy. He was every girl's dream. He was very outspoken and he influenced Chioma greatly to become lively and friendly. Before they met, Chioma was a snub and unfriendly fellow who always stayed on her lane. Those girls who had been tripping for Donald became jealous of Chioma when they found out that his heart was beating for her. Ironically, Chioma was dense about Donald's feelings for her mainly because she did not want any distraction. She only wanted them to be casual friends with good understanding.

'Bestie, we are going to Chitis straight away because I'm curious to know what has made you become the shadow of yourself overnight. I can't keep calm any longer.' Donald held Chioma's hand and led her out of the classroom without her objecting. She was feeling better now that she had someone who would insist on finding out what was wrong with her even when she proved stubborn. She instantly became emotional because she felt loved.

Chitis was one of the biggest eateries on campus. Some students went there to relax after a hectic day while some went there to gossip or gist about the latest happenings in school. Many students patronised Chitis during Student Union Government (SUG) elections, Faculty, and Departmental elections. Some of the election candidates took some people who mattered out and spoiled them with Chitis delicacies to secure their full support. Some also went there to hold meetings and, in the end, patronise the eatery for refreshments.

At the eatery, Chioma refused to eat anything, but Donald insisted that they would not have any discussion until both of them ate something. Chioma was happy seeing Donald displaying that aspect of him, yet she pretended not to care. She realized that what she needed at the moment was who would show her true love without expecting anything from her. She saw Donald as a rock to rely on. After much pretense and attention-seeking from Donald, she agreed to eat fried rice and eat with him. Donald was enjoying every bit of the time he spent with Chioma; he was glad that he had the privilege of having her full attention.

'Donald, now you have won, let me tell you what is wrong with me,' Chioma told him. She ignored Donald who was impatiently waiting for her to tell him what was happening and concentrated on picking some grains of rice that had fallen on the table while she was eating back to her plate. After that, she called a waiter to come and carry their plates before she continued talking.

'Dear Donald, you know I haven't hidden anything from you since we became friends. You have equally influenced me and you know that. You are truly a good friend to me and you have been of help to me but sincerely, I made up my mind to solve my problems this time around without involving anyone. I did not want to bother you either but since you have insisted on knowing what troubles me, I will tell you.' Chioma was already emotional as she opened up to him. They were sitting opposite each other; Donald stretched his hands on the table and took Chioma's hands. As he rubbed her palms in his, she felt relieved and comfortable.

'It all started last month when my mum refused to allow me rest. Within a week, she had already given three of her friends' sons my phone number. She was expecting me to choose one of the men to be my husband. According to her, she wanted me to marry before I graduate so that my season of marriage would not pass. Again, I found out that some guys were seriously stalking me. Every day a guy will stop me on the road and start spouting nonsense. It was on the last day I went to night class, it then that the Boss, popularly known as Viper, approached me after scaring the hell out of me, and told me that he was the one sending his guys to stalk me. He had to come himself to let me know what he was feeling for me. You needed to see how his eyes lasciviously scanned my body that night.

'When it was 5 am, I quickly told him that we would continue our discussion the next time I came for night class but that day was my last night in a night class. The last straw that broke the camel's back was when Dr Eze and Dr Udo threatened to give me a grade C in their course if I failed to give them what they wanted. Dr Eze nearly made love to me in his office… Don't give me that look again, Donald. I did not tell you before going to their office that day because you weren't in school; it was on the day you were sick,' Chioma narrated everything to him with tears in her eyes.

Donald was already boiling with anger. He managed to wait for Chioma to finish what she was saying.

'Bestie, this is unfair. You were going through all these alone, yet, refused to tell me your friend. That's not the issue now; you will apologize to me later. As for that so-called Viper, do not worry about him harming you. My father, the school authorities, and some respected personnel in UNN had a meeting yesterday and they concluded on forcefully expelling Viper and his gangs from school and it will happen sooner than you expected. That Viper guy has bitten more than he can chew. I also heard that last three days, the guy and his gang raped four first years who attempted leaving the night class venue before 5 am. Leaving these kinds of so-called students in UNN is a suicidal mission because they will end up victimizing all the students in this school and lecturers will also not be spared. The school authority has decided to forcefully expel him and his gang from the school since his father failed to call him to order even after promising the school severally to make his son change.' Donald confidently stated.

'These two lecturers have started this their madness again. They can never learn their lessons,' he continued, 'even after being punished by the department when a student reported them for molesting her in the office. This time around, I will personally see that they go down for this. I don't mind the length I will go to teach them their lessons a hard way. I will never rest until I see their self-destruction.' Donald threatened fiercely. Murderous aura was emitting from Donald. Chioma was a bit frightened because she had never seen her friend so angered. Donald later asked her whether she had evidence against those lecturers and he was glad that she recorded Dr Eze and Dr Udo's threat.

After the tense conversation, they moved on to jesting about their course-mates' reactions over her sudden solitary attitude. She found out that the number of people who went to Donald to enquire what Chioma's problem was far greater than the ones who came to her directly. In the middle of their conversation, they forgot themselves and were carried away with self-admiration. Just like two love birds, they were gazing at each other. Donald wondered why Chioma had refused to date him even when he knew that both of them had the same feelings for each other. He had invited her countless times to his family house to meet his parents but Chioma kept saying no. Chioma's refusal to be in a serious relationship with Donald made his feelings for her stronger.

The thought of saying good night to Chioma annoyed Donald. He only wanted to take Chioma home and make sure she was okay. What he felt for her at the moment was what he had never felt for any girl before. This made him start questioning himself to know whether what he was feeling for her was love or lust. On the other hand, Chioma was wondering why her feelings for Donald was rising fast. For the first time, she felt like being in Donald's arms. She felt like telling Donald to kiss her. She restrained herself from making any move that would send signals to Donald, but her eyes betrayed her. Love and emotion were boldly written in her eyes. Chioma was glad that they were not in a lonely place because she would have personally initiated a kiss with the way she was feeling. Still, she wished everyone would leave the eatery so that both of them would be left alone and she would be free to kiss Donald's lovely pink lips. She noticed that even as dark as Donald was, he still had lovely pink lips.

Before Chioma knew what was happening, Donald had taken her right hand and kissed the back of the hand passionately. He stood from his seat and went to her side. He planted a kiss on her forehead but her eyes were already closed when she saw his mouth coming close to her. He saw that Chioma did not fight back but he did not proceed because he did not know what she wanted at that moment and the presence of some students around them incapacitated him. This made her embarrassed but she concealed her embarrassment and pretended as if nothing happened.

He accompanied her back to her hostel that was not far from the eatery. Both of them kept mute on their way to her hostel. Before Donald bade her farewell, they found themselves hugging tightly. The hug lasted for some minutes before they separated.

*****   *****   *****

Donald took the bull by the horns as he had promised Chioma. With his father's support, he reported Dr Eze and Dr Udo in all the offices that mattered using the phone recording as evidence against them. Donald knew that reporting the case in only one office might cause justice to be repudiated or deterred, so he took it upon himself to report the case to many offices that mattered. He made himself vulnerable to those lecturers who were in the same business with Dr Eze and Dr Udo.

After much investigation and query, Dr Eze and Dr Udo were suspended from the school for three years without salary. The news about those two lecturers spread like wildfire on the campus and they were humiliated. Their reputations were not spared either. This made all academic and non-academic staff that had skeletons in their cupboards behave themselves properly. Students were mandated to report any case of sexual harassment from any lecturer without delay or fear. Donald became more prominent in school after this incident; he was esteemed by both students and lecturers.

Just like Donald told Chioma earlier, Viper and his gangs were rusticated from school. Those bad guys thought that they had become above the law of the University until the school authority mobilised Enugu State Militants that arrested all of them during their last riot attempt. After their rustication from school, UNN knew incredible peace. Students started going to night class voluntarily without fear of them being attacked on the road or being raped. Despite this progress, however, Chioma still refused to attend night classes again because she was afraid that there might still be Viper's look-alikes waiting for her somewhere to take revenge on her.

Because of the popularity of Donald, everybody started referring to Chioma as his girlfriend; you hardly saw any of them without seeing the other close. Chioma became the envy of most female students in their faculty who wished that Donald would acknowledge them one day especially some of her third year course mates who felt that every guy in their clad wanted to date Chioma. Chioma had some fans whose dreams were to become like her one day, especially first-year and second-year students who took her as their role model. She organized free tutorials for first-year and second-year students in her department once a week, respectively. She also organized revision class for some of her interested course mates before the beginning of every semester exam. There were still some students who also wished that Chioma would contest for Miss UNN; she was very beautiful in all areas.

Thursdays were usually the best days for third-year students in the Mass Communication department because their lectures often ended before noon and Fridays were their lecture-free days. Some students who sponsored themselves in school used those days to engage in their respective businesses. Some others saw those days as their flirting days — they would leave the campus and come back on Sunday for Monday's lectures. Other sets of people saw those days as their resting days; they would joyfully rest from Thursday to Sunday. The bookworms made up of those who engaged those days in studying as if their lives depended on studying. Every third-year student in Mass Communication looked forward to seeing Thursday for various reasons.

It was Thursday and lectures had ended for Chioma. After exchanging pleasantries with some of her course mates, she headed straight to the departmental library to check for some recommended texts. Donald followed her as usual; he signaled her to stop when she was about to open the departmental library door.

'Bestie, you know you will not be absent from my birthday party on Sunday at Old Carolina Hotel?' Donald asked rhetorically.

Chioma was taken aback by what Donald said to her. She had never attended any party in UNN, not even a birthday party. She wondered how Donald would have the mind to invite her to Old Carolina Hotel for a birthday party. She had not gone to the hotel before but she had heard her roommates talk about the hotel.

'Donald, how could you invite me to Old Carolina for your birthday party? You know perfectly well that I don't fancy attending a party of any sort. Of all places to celebrate your birthday, you chose Old Carolina, a hotel? I wonder if you are expecting me to honor the invitation or to wish you a happy birthday in advance.' Chioma was stunned.

Donald tried his best to talk Chioma into honoring his invitation. He assured her of tight security and comfort. He also promised to pick her from her hostel and bring her back after the party ended or lodge her in the hotel since Monday was a public holiday. After much convincing and persuasion, Chioma agreed to honor the invitation since it was Donald's first time celebrating his birthday in a big way.

'Alright! By God's grace, I will attend the party but on the condition that you will tell the M.C not to introduce me as your girlfriend. I do not want to be noticed.' Chioma teased him. She also told him that another condition for her coming was that he would bring her back to her hostel before 10 pm which was the time her hostel closed the gates.

'Bestie, you know there are no way you will not be introduced as my girlfriend. It's very unfair, I have been asking you out for almost a year now but you keep dashing my hope on the floor. It doesn't matter to me any longer because everybody knows you as my girlfriend, and you and I also know very well that you are mine. My church girl, I know you will attend both church and fellowship on Sunday but please be back on time because I will come and pick you by 7:30 pm,' Donald said and motioned her to open the library door and enter. Without objection, Chioma happily entered the library to study while Donald told her that he would join her in a short while.

FIVE

It was already Sunday evening, and Chioma was busy ransacking her wardrobe to find the best cloth to wear for Donald's birthday party. She did everything she proposed to do for the day except go to School's library that evening to study. She felt going to the library would make her not have ample time to prepare for the event. She was eager to attend the party and desired to look her best.

Chioma could not understand why she was excited at the thought of being Donald's close friend. She was afraid to think she was falling in love with Donald because she was not ready to be in a committed relationship with him; she preferred to be just his close friend. Yet, her feelings for Donald constantly betrayed her each time she thought of Donald as just her casual friend. Recently, she had begun to feel like welcoming Donald's kiss if he made any attempt to do so. She smiled when she remembered the resounding slap she gave him the day he attempted kissing her in the class only two of them had been in the class reading after the day's lecture.

She woke from her deep thought when her eyes spotted her yellow gown hanging at the end of her wardrobe. She remembered the day she bought the gown from Ogige Market. She had not worn it anywhere since she bought it because the gown was short, stopping mid-thigh. She saw the gown neatly hung at the seller's shop and she liked it and fortunately for her, she had come to the market to buy some clothes. She quickly bargained for it and bought it with some other clothes. When she reached her hostel, she found out that the gown was above her knee level and she hated wearing any cloth that was not at least knee-length. But, she also couldn't give the gown out because it was fine and more costly than the other clothes she bought that day.

She brought the gown out and wore it. She went to the other side of the room to check herself on the huge mirror in her room, pleased with her reflection in the mirror. Her voluptuous hips, pointed buttocks, and medium-sized breasts occupied the gown which emphasized the nice shape of her flat tummy. To assuage her guilt, she constantly reassured herself several times that she did not look seductive but beautiful. Chioma was sad that none of her roommates was around to compliment her look. It was her 6 pm alarm that made her realize that she didn't have the whole time to stand idly. Taking off her dress, she took her bucket of water and hurried to the bathroom to bathe. Knowing that she would spend some time putting on little make-up on her face, she quickly took her bath.

Chioma was raring and ready to go when her phone rang and she saw that it was Donald calling her. She didn't bother to pick the call. She knew that Donald would be waiting outside her hostel, so she locked her room door and left instantly.

She stepped out of her hostel cat walking like a model. Her face was glowing; light make-up had always fit her face even though she didn't like wearing makeup except on special occasions. Her height was doubled because of the three-inch high heels she was wearing. Her black heels fit her black, fancy handbag. Her long, human-hair weave was let loose at her back. The sunshades she was putting on also made her face more beautiful and not easily recognized.

Donald could not believe his eyes when he saw Chioma stepping out of her hostel in style. He was carried away by Chioma's beauty and forgot to let Chioma know where he was. He had never seen her dressed like that before; he began to have the usual body sensation. He came back to his senses when he saw Chioma bring out her phone and was scrolling; about to dial someone's number. He quickly opened the car door and came out from his brand new Camry, smiling at Chioma who was directly opposite him. It was then that Chioma saw that it was Donald. He majestically walked to her like a groom going to meet his bride.

Chioma instantly felt underdressed seeing how expensive Donald looked. Both of them hugged not minding the students loitering in front of the hostel. The love birds drew the attention of most female students doing one thing or the other in front of the hostel; they stared at them and blushed on their behalf. Donald led her to the other side of the car and opened the front door for her. The attention on her was much, she felt like the most important person on earth at that particular time.

The car was a black Camry with tinted glasses. Donald's dad had promised to officially hand the car over to him after his final year project defence. He was afraid that the car would be a distraction to his son if he handed it over to him in his third year. After much pleading from Donald's mum and him, his father agreed to allow him to drive the car on his birthday with the condition that he would not drive it again until the right time.

Chioma was never expecting Donald to come with a car so she felt she needed to ask him about the car before he zoomed off.

'Dad bought a car for me but he said that the car will officially be mine after our final year project defence because he was afraid of his son being distracted,' Donald explained to Chioma as if he read her thoughts.

'Your dad is right. You have to be patient and finish your degree first. Your car is very fine and you aren't looking bad at all.' Chioma complimented him.

Donald did not stop complimenting Chioma on their way to the venue of the party. He later summoned the courage to tell Chioma what had been on his mind for some time now. He pleaded with her to give her the privilege of lodging her in Old Carolina Hotel as his honorable guest. After much debate, Chioma agreed and told him to promise her that nothing would go wrong for any reason.

Old Carolina Hotel was one of the popular hotels in Nsukka. It was not far from the Campus, about a two-minute drive from UNN and a five-minute drive from Nsukka Central Park. It was named after the owner. It had various halls like the multi-purpose hall, executive bar, fitness centre, and a restaurant. There was a twenty-four-hour light supply in the hotel, coupled with tight security. It also boasted a point-and-kill and relaxation spot. Minet cable TV, Cab services, and Laundry services were rendered.

Donald had booked the executive bar that night for his twenty-fifth birthday party. Before Donald and Chioma arrived, the venue was already filled with Donald's friends, some of his course mates, and fans. The number of Donald's invitees multiplied by two because almost every one of them came with either a girlfriend or boyfriend. Donald was not taken aback by the large turn up because he had expected it. It was a norm for students to attend functions, especially night functions, with their partners.

Thus, before that day, he had made extra provisions for his uninvited guests.

***** ***** *****

'Donald, you spent money on this your birthday party,' Chioma complimented Donald when she came out of the bathroom; drying her face with the edge of the towel she tied carefully to avoid the towel from letting loose. Many wrapped gifts were scattered on the floor and Donald was opening them one after the other to see what was in them when he heard Chioma's voice. He turned to where Chioma was standing and became lost in thought.

'You don't have to get lost. Stop staring at me like that because you are making me uncomfortable. Give me some privacy or do you want me to leave the room for you?' Chioma snapped him.

He immediately apologized to Chioma for making her feel uncomfortable, stating that he couldn't resist looking at the beautiful damsel standing before him.

'Bestie, I have not celebrated my birthday in the past ten years now so dad and mum decided to celebrate my birthday for me in a grand style. Dad said that his son has turned twenty-five which means that he has become a full-grown man.' Donald chuckled.

'Mum and dad tried for you. Food and drinks were in surplus, and everything was in place,' Chioma stated. Her mood changed when she saw the nightgown Donald kept on the bed for her.

When Donald saw her reaction to the nightgown, he asked her why she stared at it as if it scared her. She kept quiet for some time before responding to him because she did not want to be rude to him.

'Donald, I can't wear this. I don't know where on earth you got this thing you call nightgown. Don't you see how short and transparent it is? Anyway, there's no cause for alarm because you will have to book another room for yourself if you want me to wear it. After all, I can't wear it and sleep in the same room with you,' Chioma angrily told him.

Donald did not argue with her because he knew she was determined not to wear the nightgown he bought for her. He calmly told her to suit herself and wear the gown she wore to the party since she did not sweat much. She had refused to dance at the party and was under air-conditioning all through. Donald left the room for some time to give her some privacy.

He went back to the executive bar which was not far from the room he booked for himself and Chioma.

Fortunately for him, he saw two of his male course mates still having a nice time with their girlfriends. He joined them and after jesting with them for a while, they offered him a glass of wine. He refused to drink it because he didn't like taking alcoholic drinks but they insisted he drank it to prove that he was man enough. After much persuasion, he drank a glass of the wine they offered him. Shortly after, he became dizzy, so he excused himself and went back to the room.

Chioma opened the door for him when she heard his voice calling her. He entered the bathroom straightaway and had his bath. He came out of the bathroom after freshening up and joined her on the bed.

Chioma used the two pillows on the bed to create a demarcation between her side and Donald's side. The two pillows were carefully placed on the duvet in such a way that one could comfortably lie under it without shifting the pillows. Donald thought that Chioma was already asleep; she faced the wall and her back was turned to his side. He carefully removed the pillows, kept one for himself, and raised Chioma's head gently, and placed the other under her head. Donald turned and faced the other side of the room which made Chioma think that he was asleep already.

Chioma had desired to sleep in a hotel room because she had never slept in one before Donald's birthday party. She had seen many pictures of hotel rooms on the internet and had been eager to experience the calmness and comfort that came with lodging in one. When Donald pleaded with her to allow him to lodge her in Old Carolina Hotel, she agreed because she had desired to sleep in a hotel and know what it was like.

Suddenly, she didn't understand why she lost her peace. Sleep disappeared from her eyes and for the first time, she regretted allowing Donald to lodge her in that hotel. She began to imagine what would become of her if Donald who was currently playing a gentleman turned into a beast later in the night. She blamed herself for ever agreeing to be in the same room and on the same bed with Donald.

Chioma slept off amidst her thoughts and was woken when she felt someone's hand unzipping her gown. She didn't realize that he had come close to her because she was fast asleep. She quickly jumped down from the bed, went to the door, and stood there. Even though she dated Donald with her eyes, her mind was far from having intimacy with him. She was thinking about what next to do since leaving the room might be dangerous for her. Donald lustfully stared at her for some seconds before going close to her.

'Donald, don't try anything funny with me. Just stay back and don't dare come close to me or you will regret tonight.'

Donald ignored her terrorizing voice and continued his advances. Chioma knew she was making an empty threat but that was the only option left for her at the moment. Donald walked past her and went to the light switch that was behind her and switched it off. He went back to the bed and sat down. Donald did not want to do anything that both of them would regret later so he did his best to control his emotions, a feat that proved abortive. He stood again and went to where Chioma was still standing. Giving up, he grabbed her and gave her a passionate, long kiss to prevent her from uttering another word. Donald gently led her to the bed when he saw that she succumbed to his advances. He stretched his hands to turn on AC before he covered their bodies with the duvet.

The pleasure Donald was giving her at the moment made her initial fear and worry swiftly disappear. She stopped struggling and allowed Donald had his way. She quickly silenced the voice accusing her of losing her virginity. It had always been her dream to be deflowered by her husband on their wedding night, but the fire Donald ignited in her was unquenchable. Donald successfully unlocked her garden. Her feelings for Donald did not start that night but was intensified. She placed her head on Donald's chest and slept off after two successful rounds of sex.

SIX

'Donald, stop pestering me or I will show you the worst part of me. I guess you won't like to see that beastly side of me.' Chioma snapped rudely.

Donald pleaded with Chioma to give him a second chance to prove to her that he had become a better person for good but Chioma paid no attention to him and left angrily.

After Donald had carnal knowledge of Chioma on his birthday, he avoided her like a plague. He managed to drop Chioma in her hostel the next morning. Throughout the drive home, he kept mute, giving her the cold shoulder. Donald was moody throughout the whole day but was careful enough to pretend to be alright around his mother.

He was relieved that the following day, Monday, was a public holiday. He wanted to have enough time to be alone without seeing Chioma, to gather enough courage to face Chioma. Unfortunately for Donald, he lost his appetite for Chioma's voice within those two days of self-isolation. When he got to the department the next day, he intentionally went to the departmental library and stayed there, intending to enter the class the moment other students arrived.

Before Donald's birthday, both he and Chioma usually reserved seats for one another when any of them came to school first. They weren't known for late coming either. Whenever any of their classmates saw a sitting space near Chioma or Donald, the person needed not to ask for the owner of the space because they regularly sat beside each other. In line with this, Chioma reserved a seat for Donald until it became clear to her that he was intentionally avoiding her. She initially thought that Donald had developed the habit of coming late to lectures without knowing that he stayed at the departmental library every day he came to school in order not to be forced to sit beside her. Donald also developed the attitude of leaving the class, sometimes through the back door, before the end of lectures so that Chioma would not talk to him.

After a while, Chioma became tired of calling Donald on the phone because he kept busying her calls. Before his birthday, he was the one calling her every day to hear from her but after his birthday, the reverse became the case. Chioma's efforts to find out what was wrong with him were met with a rebuttal as he ignored her each time she reached out to him. It wasn't long before their course mates carried the rumor that the love birds had broken up. Out of frustration and bitterness, Chioma made up her mind to let go of Donald.

Faculty and departmental exams were usually written under one week, and General Studies (GS) courses were written, sometimes two weeks or one month after the faculty and departmental exams. Some students whose family houses were not far from the campus would travel home and go back to school some days before the GS exams or go to the exam hall straight from their house. However, other students that resided very far from school would stay around and wait to write GS or their last papers before travelling.

The students also had different perspectives on the waiting period. While some saw the waiting period as a time to flirt, others embraced the mindset that GS courses were very simple because it was CBT. Ironically, most of them kept failing woefully without learning their lessons; they only learnt their lessons when they discovered that the so-called simple GS had made them have extra years in school.

Chioma studied for her forthcoming exams like never before. She put her emotions aside knowing well that she had a target. Instead of being drained by the bitterness and frustration, Donald caused her; she channeled the energy towards her books. She stayed in school two weeks after the end of both faculty, departmental, and GS exams before travelling to Anambra to spend the long vacation with her family. Meanwhile, his thoughts continually reverberated around her mind when she was at home. She discovered that she had not gotten over Donald's love, care, and concern. Part of her wished that Donald would come back to her and apologize to her. Soon enough started wishing for another experience of what happened between her and Donald at the Old Carolina Hotel that night. She became more battered when she remembered how Donald had soon moved on with a second-year student who was also in their department, fanning the flames of jealousy in her heart. She constantly cried her eyes out whenever she was left alone in the house. Chioma thought that Donald would not be able to stay without her but she was proved wrong. She kept hoping that he would call her phone number one day but it never happened.

The Mass Communication department assigned project supervisors to her third-year students before they travelled for a long vacation. Professor Akwanya was a principled man who believed in doing the right things at the right time. He hated it when his supervisees hurried him to go through their works to follow their mates and defend, which was why he insisted that his supervisees submit the first chapter of their project to him for correction before they travel home. Before the end of the first semester of final year, Professor Akwanya's supervisees would be rounding off their works. Chioma was glad that her project supervisor, Professor Akwanya, insisted on his supervisees submitting their rough work on chapters one and two before travelling. To meet up, she stayed two weeks in school after the exam before travelling home. The fact that her project supervisor corrected her works and instructed her on how to go about it made her happier.

One unique thing about Chioma was that she always converted her pains to energy to do anything her mind was on especially academic works. She spent most of her time at home researching her project topic. She made sure she never missed Sunday services for any reason so that her parents would not query her or suspect that she was hiding something from them. She attended weekly, church activities sometimes and used her project as an excuse for other times she failed to attend.

When the new academic session started, Chioma resumed school having resolved in her heart never to think about Donald again, reserved seats for him, or look out for him.

One faithful evening, when Chioma was returning to her hostel from the library, a new clean Mercedes Benz stopped beside her. Her initial thought was that the person inside the car wanted to ask her for directions, so she stopped to answer. Then, a young man in his late thirties rolled the tinted glass down to enable Chioma to see his face. When their eyes met, he gave Chioma a beaming smile which made her diffident. The first thing the man told her before introducing himself was that she was beautiful. He introduced himself as John Chukwudi, a businessman from Abia State who came to Enugu for a business contract that would last for a year. He told her that he had entered the campus to see one of his old-time friends who was a lecturer in the Chemistry department. After a little persuasion, Chioma agreed to give him her phone number.

Enugu is the capital of Enugu State. It was more developed than other towns in Enugu State. Nsukka was rated the second most developed town in Enugu State because of the number one university the first Nigerian Governor founded there shortly after the country's independence.

Afterwards, John started calling Chioma on the phone as if his whole life depended on him hearing her voice. Initially, she detested how often John called her but soon grew to enjoy his frequent calls and the time she spent with him. Because John was a busy man, he promised to visit her in school every Saturday to spend some time with her a fact that pleased her. Despite her growing attraction, she didn't want to trade her study time for anything.

Whenever John visited, he stayed with Chioma for about an hour before going back to Enugu. This gave her enough time to study and work on her project without flagging. John always made sure he brought gifts or provisions for Chioma whenever he visited. Within a short time, they soon became close friends and she told him everything about herself.

John showed her practical love: he didn't only profess his love for her but his actions said everything. This, he left Chioma with no other option than to reciprocate his love. He never relented in crediting Chioma's bank account even without her requesting for it. She soon focused on his affection, forgetting, with time, that there was once a person called Donald in her life.

The first semester ended faster than anyone could imagine; it had always been like that because of the short period. This time Chioma did not travel for the two-week break given to them after her final year first semester exams ended. Some other students did not travel because their house was very far from school.

Chioma did not travel because she wanted to make sure her project was ready before the beginning of the second semester. It was then that John started visiting her on Fridays and Sundays. Chioma did not feel the pain of not travelling home because of John's company. He also provided everything she needed for her. Chioma's parents became worried at a point that their daughter was no longer calling them for money but she told them that she was spending the little money she had saved over time. Sometimes, her parents stopped waiting for her to ask for money; they sent money to her sometimes without her asking for it.

When the final year second semester resumed, Donald started showing interest in Chioma again but it was already late for him because her mind was made up against him. Donald begged Chioma several times for forgiveness but the more he pleaded with her, the more hardened her heart became. His actions seemed like one who had drunk a love potion. Donald often waited after lectures to plead with Chioma to forgive him because that was the only time he could speak with her; she had stopped answering whenever he called her on phone. She had blocked him on social media and also blocked his two phone numbers.

'Bestie, please find a place in your heart to forgive me of my many sins. I'm sorry for all wrong I have done,' Donald pleaded with Chioma but she ignored him and left.

SEVEN

John Chukwudi sat in his car thinking about how to convince his wife not to visit him next week at Enugu. After seeing Chioma in school that Saturday, she had promised to come to his house next week Saturday. He was excited that Chioma finally agreed to visit him after much waiting. Unfortunately for John, his wife insisted on visiting him with their children on Friday and going back to Lagos on Monday.

John and his family were living in Lagos happily before he was given a business contract by Enugu's Governor. His companies at Abuja, and Lagos the headquarters, manufactured plumbing materials like adaptor, barb, coupling, cross, double-tapped bushing, elbow, mechanical sleeve, nipple, plug and cap, reducer, tee, union, valve, and wyes. John embodied a man who got established on time. At thirty-eight he had already established two popular, plumbing-material companies in Lagos and Abuja.

Governor Chika Ezema was one of his close friends from the time he schooled at the University of Ibadan, Oyo State. When Governor Chika Ezema contested during elections, John carried the campaign with zeal and much zest. It was John who gave Governor Chika half of the money he spent during his contest. This, when Governor Chika won the election, he decided to give John a one-year business contract to supply plumbing materials for the building of the government estate at Enugu, as a gesture of appreciation.

Back at home, John's wife soon began to worry over her husband's refusal to come and visit them, not minding that his children were missing him. His two boys were three and five years old respectively. John had promised his wife before coming to Enugu that he would be visiting them every month but failed to keep his promise, five months later. After many attempts by his wife to persuade her husband to visit them failed, she resorted to paying him a visit with their children.

John believed that a woman didn't need to work as long as her husband could provide for all her needs. This mindset made him refuse his wife to work after they got married. His wife who was a practicing nurse in one of the state hospitals before she got married to him, battled with him for five years before he allowed her to start working in one of the private hospitals close to their house. John insisted that his wife would register their boys in the hospital's school so that her eyes would be on them, seeing that the hospital's Nursery, Primary and Secondary school was one of the best schools in the whole of Lagos State.

'I don't have any other option than to tell Chioma that I have an important meeting to attend at Lagos next week. I don't want my wife to know my house here before she pays me a surprise visit one day that may spoil things for me. Yes, Chioma has to wait. Besides, I have been pleading with her to visit me but she kept refusing. She finally agreed to visit me next weekend but my wife has insisted on visiting me too next weekend with my children. My wife first before I consider any other person.' John thought before zooming off from the campus.

*****   *****   *****

'Baby, I am delighted you have forgiven me. The meeting I attended at Lagos last weekend was urgent and I had to be there, despite the short notice. I seriously wanted us to spend that last weekend together but that meeting became a hindrance to the wonderful weekend I planned for us. Thank you once again for knowing that I did not choose the impromptu meeting over you,' John professed piquantly as he opened the door for Chioma to enter.

Chioma was swept off her feet by John's continued apology for postponing her visit to his house because of the emergency meeting he attended last weekend. She was glad that she had found true love.

'It's alright dear, I understand that you are a businessman and that is one attribute of businessmen.' Chioma giggled before entering the house.

A pair of imposing bookcases climbed to the top of each side of an enormous alcove, with an ornate framed mirror hanging at the center of the wall which glowed. The arrangement of the modern chandelier used various sizes and forms to create what looked like an entertaining fireworks display. A modern coffee table was at the center of the living room. The living room was dominated by colorful sofas that were orderly arranged. The floor had an assumed sofa design. The living room also featured a constructed TV wall over part of the huge windows. It was painted an off-white color with flowered patterns.

'This is amazing! Outside looks like a paradise and inside is like heaven on earth; I thought I had seen it all until I saw how beautiful this place is,' Chioma said, not knowing how best to praise the magnificent building.

John chuckled and told her that she would be welcomed anytime she visited. John frequently glanced at his wristwatch as he took Chioma around the house. He showed her all the rooms in the house. He took his time to show Chioma all the bedrooms with their conveniences. He also took her to the kitchen and patiently explained how all the electrical appliances worked. Chioma was amazed at what she saw; she could not imagine that such kind of house existed in Enugu.

'Baby, I want you to feel at home. Please, dear, I have a brief meeting with the Governor this afternoon. I promise you it will be very brief. I showed you all the rooms so that you will not be afraid when I go and think I left a beast in one of the rooms that will devour you,' John said pretentiously.

Chioma chuckled, replying that she trusted him and knew he had her best interests at heart.

John had resolved in his heart before bringing Chioma from campus to his house that he would give her an excuse that would make him go and leave her in the house. He decided to trick Chioma because she insisted earlier that he would bring her back to the hostel the same day but he wanted her to sleepover in his house. Thus, he planned to return late, leaving her with no option but to sleep. Before he left he told her to cook anything she wanted and eat without waiting for him because he would eat at the meeting.

After John left, Chioma quickly went to the kitchen to prepare noodles and eggs for herself because she was hungry. When she finished cooking, she sat on the floor and rushed her food so that John would not come back and see her eating like a hungry lioness. She made sure she washed everything she cooked with and kept them back carefully. After eating, she went back to the sitting room and made herself comfortable on one of the sofas. She kept herself busy with her phone, waiting for his return. Because she didn't like to watch movies, she avoided the television and did not bother changing the channel since she did not find the remote.

When it was getting late, Chioma tried several times to call John on the phone but her calls were unanswered. She contemplated returning to the campus but gave up that idea when she didn't find the key to the house, to enable her to lock up after she left. She felt that thieves would over power the old gatekeeper, break in and take some valuable things from the house if she left it open.

After a while, she went to the exit door and realizing that it had an inside bolt, she locked sat on the couch. Out of frustration, she slept off.

Chioma woke up when she heard a slight knock on the door. She checked her wristwatch and saw that the time was 11 pm. She was about to ask who the person was when she heard John's voice outside, telling her to open the door for him.

'For real? You are just coming back? I told you that I would not like to sleep over but see the time you are coming back. Do you expect me to go back to Nsukka now?' Chioma challenged John angrily when she opened the door for him.

Before Chioma could utter another word, John was already on his knees pleading for Chioma's forgiveness. She was shocked. She had never seen a man like John displaying such humility before a lady. She had prepared herself for his defence but was taken aback when he did the opposite. Her heart soon melted and she forgave him instantly. She raised him up and calmly asked him to tell her what happened and why he had refused to answer when she called.

John did not hide his excitement when he saw that Chioma had forgiven him, and patiently recited his well-planned explanation. 'Baby, the meeting lingered more than I expected. It was a meeting with the Governor so I was unable to leave before the meeting ended. Other business associates were also there and it would not be right for me to start answering calls there because it was an official meeting. Besides, it's against our ethics to bring out our phones during meetings so I put my phone on silent mode and did not know when you called. I'm sorry, we were debating on a delicate matter so I was not able to excuse myself and call you to inform you of the development,' John deceitfully explained to her. He also told her that the reason she perceived alcohol on from his body because was that was what they were served with as refreshment in the meeting.

John did not go for any meeting but to their business partner's house who was also his friend. They both drank to stupor as he waited for night to come before going back to his house. Sadly, Chioma did not sense his deceit because she trusted him. She jokingly told him that he was stinking that he should go and freshen up first. He obeyed her without objection just like a son would obey his mother.

John smiled to himself all through like a boy who had just won a trophy for the first time. After bathing, he wore small pants that revealed the shape of his body, and his chest was bare which exposed his nicely shaped upper body. He went to the living room and joined Chioma. He pretended not to know that she was embarrassed by his appearance. However, he saw how she shyly turned her face to another side when she saw him.

'Baby, do you mind freshening up?' John asked her, but she told him she did not want to bathe again because she took her bath before coming. He did not argue with her. Rather, he took the television remote from where it was kept and sat close to her. While he pretended to be engrossed with surfing the channel, she ignored his living, breathing presence in the room, although she was aware of every move he made.

After finally choosing a channel that currently showed wrestling, John cleared his throat which made Chioma turn look at him.

'Baby, don't be afraid, I'm fine. It is just that I want to tell you that I will be travelling to Lagos next weekend because my company there needs my attention. I will come back after a month,' John told Chioma.

She did not know when she shouted, 'A month?' She could not imagine a month without seeing John.

John had informed his wife two days ago about his one month leave from work and his wife told him to spend the one month with his family in Lagos. He initially wanted to give his wife an excuse why he would not spend that one month at Lagos but decided against it when he realized how much he had missed his children.

'Baby, do not worry, we will keep in touch, although not often because of the workload. I may not be able to call you often or answer your call always but whenever I have the opportunity, I will not hesitate to call you. You know you are the only one I care for. It's just a matter of four weeks and I will be back to my sweet baby,' He said, trying to pacify her.

When John saw that Chioma was already emotional, he carefully put her head on his chest. Soon, he started playing with her hair. After a short time, he whispered something to Chioma which made her remove her head from his chest.

'It's okay if you are not interested but I'm thinking it will be a good thing for us to have a memory that will keep a smile on our faces for this period of one month when we will be far from each other. You know I have not asked you for anything before so if you do this for me, not even for me but for the sake of love we share, it will be very good,' John told her passionately, which made her more emotional.

'Sweetheart, it is not that I want to deny you the only thing you have ever asked me to do. I want us to be very close more than you can imagine but it is just that, after the first mistake I made, I promised myself to remain zipped up until I marry,' Chioma uttered persistently.

'It's obvious you don't want to be the mother of my unborn kids. There is no problem, I'm okay with that. But I thought you knew better than this. I would like us to be together forever. I have studied you and my findings show that you are a woman of noble character, a woman of strong will, and you are too lovely. I also see you as a good wife to her husband.' John praised her.

Chioma blushed as she asked John whether the praise was supposed to be a marriage proposal.

'Let me use the word 'yes',' John chuckled and brought Chioma's head close to his chest again.

Driven with lust, he soon started caressing her breasts and said to her, 'Please allow these breasts to breastfeed my prince and princess.'

Helpless with desire, Chioma succumbed to his advances and released herself wholly to John, even as he took her to his bedroom. Chioma had promised herself never to have sex again until her wedding night but it was as if Donald had activated an unavoidable sexual urge in her the first time she had intimacy with him. She silenced her conscience that told her that she was doing the wrong thing with the claim that John had already proposed to her. She was biting her lips to suppress her moaning but the way John was touching all her sensitive parts with his tongue and hand made her moan out loudly. When she saw that the romance was already intense, she motioned for John to use protection but it was already late for him to stop. When they had finished exploring each other's bodies to their satisfaction, he had sex with her and both of them slept off.

John gave her enough money the next morning, which was Saturday, before dropping her at her hostel. He told Chioma to endeavor to make him proud as she would be defending her degree project in less than three weeks.

When Chioma saw that John's attitude towards her did not change after what happened between them the previous night, she felt a strong connection between them. The thought of John giving her an official engagement ring and coming to her house to see her parents for the marriage rites filled her heart with joy. She had planned her wedding in her heart and had also selected some of her course courses who would be in her bridal train. She knew that her parents would be happy if she got married to a tycoon like John.

EIGHT

John kept his promise to Chioma; he made sure he called her at least once a day and constantly sent money for her upkeep every weekend. These special treatments made her think that she was the only woman in John's life. She was that eager to be called John's wife officially. Unfortunately, John was only passing the time and having fun with her.

After Chioma's project defense, her health suddenly degenerated. She developed a fever and always felt sick in the morning. She kept taking a pain reliever to subside the fever but the sickness persisted. She was later advised to run a test before treatment would be given to her when she went to the school's clinic for treatment. She ran a test that instant. When the result came out the next day, she realized that she was twenty-eight days pregnant. She accepted the result with mixed feelings. Even though she desired to be John's wife, she did not want to become pregnant for him before the wedding.

Chioma did not want to break the good news on the phone for John so she kept it to herself. She was tempted to tell John but she patiently held her peace knowing that he would be back in two days. John had earlier told her to come to Enugu International Airport and welcome him. This made her more excited and happier. She constantly reassured herself that John was not ashamed to flaunt her to the whole world as his potential wife-to-be.

*****   *****   *****

'Baby, I have missed you so much. At a point, I found out I could no longer concentrate on what I was doing at Lagos because my whole mind was on coming back to see you. You know you mean the whole world to me,' John praised her.

They had just entered the house and Chioma was helping him to remove his tie when he asked her the question. Chioma knew that John was not expecting an answer from her; he had asked her the same question when they were still at the airport.

'I know I mean the whole world to you and more than the world to you. I want to say thank you for accepting me into your world. I love and respect you,' Chioma finally mumbled. She had been quiet since she saw John. Chioma only hugged him at the airport without saying a word to him, John continued the conversation. John did not even notice that Chioma had not said anything to him because he had more than a thousand words to tell her.

Chioma's heart kept beating faster as the thought of carrying John's baby kept flooding in her heart. She did not know how to open up to John; his adoration and praise did not help her too to gather courage and tell him.

She sat on one of the sofas, looking at John in admiration while he entertained her with jokes and praises. John gently pulled her up from where she was sitting and gave her a tight hug which made her less nervous. After a while, he disentangled her from his arms and both of them began to gaze into each other's eyes as if they were searching for the right way to express their emotions.

'Sweetheart, I know you called me almost every day when you were not around but it can never replace your physical presence. I think I have fallen deeply in love with you,' Chioma confessed her love for John.

John was not surprised with her love confession; he already knew that he had stolen her heart. He brought her closer to himself and said, 'I already know you have fallen deeply in love with me and that's what I want. You are my baby and you know that I have not loved you less and I will continue to love and care for you.'

Filled with this assurance, Chioma took a deep breath and gave him coquettish glances.

The atmosphere soon became charged with sexual tension as he began to kiss her and she responded to his advances. Chioma then felt it was the right time to tell John that she was carrying his baby. 'Sweetheart, there is something I want to tell you. I know you just returned from a long journey and I should have given you enough time to rest before telling anything like that but I can't curb it any longer,' Chioma fearfully told John.

John pulled her back a little to see her expression well and hear what she was afraid of saying. 'Baby, you don't need to be afraid of anything. Just tell me what the problem is. You know I will always be by your side to support you,' John told Chioma, not even hazarding a guess as to what she meant.

Chioma took a deep breath again and told John that she was pregnant for him. John's face changed instantly; sadness was written all over him. He kept mute for some seconds before distancing himself from Chioma. Chioma stared at him, surprised. She could not tell what she was expecting John to do at that particular time.

After a while, she soon regained her voice and asked him, 'Sweetheart, why are you not saying anything? Aren't you happy that I'm carrying your child or does it mean that you don't want me to be the mother of your children again?' Chioma's voice brought his absent mind back.

'Baby, what are you saying to me? I mean, why won't I be happy that my queen is carrying my child? Why won't a man be happy when he gets what he wished for? John asked her ostentatiously.

'This news calls for celebration in a grand style. Hence, I will treat you with more love and care. Let's pop Champagne first. Later in the day or tomorrow, we will throw a party and invite our friends to celebrate with us. Don't worry about people saying that a decent girl got pregnant before marriage. I will see your parents as soon as possible for our marriage arrangement,' John comforted Chioma.

He motioned her to wait for him there in the sitting room as he excitedly ran inside his bedroom. John shortly came out with two glasses of chilled juice and gave one to Chioma. She initially refused to drink the juice, her spirit unsettled at the whole situation. However, his persuasion soon wore her down as he persuaded her to drink the juice for the sake of their unborn child. She later gave in and took the juice from him and drank.

John sat beside Chioma and sipped his juice, slyly stealing glances at her from the corner of his eyes. After she had finished she stood to go to the restroom when she discovered that she could not walk because of the sharp pain she suddenly started feeling below her abdomen.

'My stomach! My stomach!' Chioma wailed in pain and collapsed on the floor. John did not say anything to her but kept looking at her without showing any reaction. Chioma kept rolling on the floor in pain, expecting John to come to her aid but it never happened. She could not say another thing because of the pain she felt.

John stood from where he was sitting and went and bolted the door. He came back and sat back; it was as if he enjoyed watching her cry in pain.

'Chioma,' John called her by her name for the first time. He continued, 'I did not want to harm you but you forced me to do so. What do you expect me to do? Marry you? You must be a joker. I knew you would have refused to abort this pregnancy that was why I did not tell you to do so. Instead, I did it my way. For your information, I'm a married man with two kids. I did not tell you because you did not care to ask me. You were only interested in my money and I made sure I gave you more than you needed. Beloved Chioma, I poisoned the juice I gave you and I doubt if you will recover from it,' John was still talking when he noticed that Chioma had faded out.

***** *****

*****

Chioma opened her eyes in a strange environment and wondered where she was. Her confusion increased when she saw the drip connected to her vein. The sharp pain she felt on her head, however, made her gave up trying to figure out where she was.

'Bestie, you are finally awake. I have been waiting for you to wake up,' Donald said passionately. He had been sitting patiently beside her bed for an hour waiting for her to wake.

Chioma turned her eyes to the direction the voice came from and noticed that someone sat beside her bed, making his face out to be Donald's. She managed to ask Donald where she was.

Donald told her that she was in the hospital. However, she refused to be satisfied with his shallow response, compelling him to tell her why she was in the hospital and everything that had happened. Chioma started crying profusely when Donald refused to answer her questions.

'Bestie, don't cry, I will tell you everything that happened,' Donald said, trying to console her. 'Three months ago, your lifeless body was found at the school gate by some security men and they alerted the school authorities immediately. You were taken to the school's clinic but after two days, you became worse so you were transferred to this hospital, the University Teaching Hospital. Two of our course mates who were receiving treatment at the school's clinic were the ones who identified your body when you were brought there and told our H. O. D. (Head of Department). Then, he insisted on you being transferred to this hospital when your state became worse at the school's clinic as a result of poor medical equipment.

'You have been in coma for three months. We had lost hope of having you alive again until last week when you suddenly started responding to treatment.

'The school authorities informed your parents when the incident occurred and they have constantly visited you. Your dad and brother always come from Anambra every weekend to see you and call often to know whether you have started responding to treatment. I have a relative who stays nearby. When I explained everything to her, she kindly gave your mum a room to stay. The hospital management had refused to allow her to sleep in the hospital. She also gave me one room since she is not married and has three bedrooms. Your mum and I usually come in the morning and go in the evening. The doctor notified your mum that you would soon be awake so she had gone to prepare food for you and she told me to stay behind.

'Upon further examination, the doctors stated that the poisonous substance found in your system flushed the baby in your womb and nearly flushed your womb too. They also said that it is very rare for someone to survive after taking the substance but all thanks to God for preserving your life.' Donald stopped talking when he saw that Chioma was already crying hysterically. He wiped her tears with his handkerchief. He consoled her and promised never to leave her again. He regretted leaving Chioma in the first place and constantly blamed himself for giving another person a chance to put Chioma in the state she was. He also asked Chioma for forgiveness again and she forgave him.

'Now that you have stopped crying, let me show you something,' Donald excitedly told Chioma, and brought out his phone from his pocket.

After searching for something on his phone, he showed Chioma the phone. Chioma's excitement instantly buried her initial sadness; joy was written all over her face.

'Congratulations, Bestie, you have made us proud. You have finally proved to everyone the stock you are made of. After all the battles fought, you won the victory at last. Nobody saw this coming except me because I know who I have got as a friend. There were many whose dreams were big and great but because they lacked the will to pursue their dreams, those great dreams remained dreams. For the few who dreamt big and their will to succeed drove them towards their dreams, not minding the rough road, in the end, their dreams became realities.

Bestie, your strong will to succeed did not just make you succeed but it made you a success. Congratulations once more, UNN's best graduating Student. It is your expectation; you worked hard for it.' Donald's joy knew no bounds. He kept praising Chioma and dancing around the hospital room.

She managed to congratulate him for also graduating with a First-Class. They were the only two who graduated with first class in their department. Donald was happier for Chioma than himself because she was the UNN BGS for the year; her CGPA was 5.0. Two companies had already sent her scholarship offers through the department to further her education in any country of her choice. Donald also knew that during the award night, Chioma would receive more offers and different kinds of gifts from different companies and individuals.

When Donald stopped dancing around, she asked him when the list was released and he told her that it was released last week. He also informed her that her people were already aware, and they were all waiting for her to get down from the sickbed so that she would be spoilt with gifts. He also told her that he had contacted someone who would work their service out so that both of them would serve in the same State. He sincerely promised her that he would never allow anyone to come between them again for any reason.

Chioma only nodded at everything Donald said. She had no strength to talk. She turned her head to the other side of the room facing the wall, and silently said a short prayer:

'Father, I know my love for you is imperfect and I have fallen short of your glory, but in your mercy, forgive me and look upon me with your eyes of perfect love. Thank you, Lord, for giving me the perfect academic end I expected. Surely, you alone did this and I'm grateful to you. I thought I would have prevailed by my strength but the storms that came my way proved my imperfection. I might have failed the test of life but, Lord, please in your perfect love perfect my imperfections. Thank You, my compassionate Father, for not forsaking me even in my unfaithfulness.'

Donald called Chioma's name three times when he became uncomfortable with her silence but when she gave him no response, he felt she had slept off. Donald went to the other side of the bed to see her face properly and he was shocked by what he saw.

Chioma's eyes were wide open without blinking, with a beaming smile on her face. He stood there for a while to know whether she would blink but she did not. He shook her body gently but she still did not respond. Donald shouted out of fear and some nurses in the ward came to know what was wrong. A doctor also rushed in. After the doctor had finished examining her, he shook his head in sorrow. They were still standing there watching Chioma lying peacefully on the hospital bed when the doctor in charge of the ward walked in. Upon further examination, he pronounced her dead and summoned the mortuary attendants to come and carry her body.

Donald was mad at the doctor when he heard him calling the mortuary attendants. In anger, he went straight to the doctor and started strangling him. One of the nurses who were also standing there immediately dialed the security emergency number. Two security men rushed in and tried to separate Donald from the doctor but it was as if Donald had the strength of a wounded lion.

The doctor was already gasping for air when Donald suddenly saw Chioma's fingers moving slightly. He left the doctor and rushed to her bed. The doctor whose eyes also trailed Donald when he suddenly left his neck equally saw Chioma's fingers moving. He quickly went over to Chioma and examined her. Before he scurried out of the ward, he dismissed the two mortuary attendants who were already standing at the ward's door, observing the events happening. He soon returned with two more doctors.

His excitement palpable, Donald looked at Chioma as if she was his lost but found treasure, and promptly obeyed when he was told to leave the ward. The doctors quickly commenced treatment on Chioma.

NINE

Chioma's house.

'My baby, please, I'm sorry for everything that happened to you. I know I caused them all.' Chioma's mother apologised to Chioma who was reading a novel at the dining table.

It had been over three months since Chioma was discharged from the hospital, asked to take adequate rest. However, her family never stopped treating her like an egg. They did not allow her to do any work, providing everything she needed.

'Mom, it's okay. I know you put me under pressure to marry but you didn't force me to make the bad decisions I made. It's already in the past. If you keep apologizing to me, I doubt the possibility of my heart being healed. It was my mistake and I have forgiven myself. My heart is still healing so don't slow my heart's healing with your unending apology,' Chioma respectfully explain to her mom.

Chioma's mom, who stood close to her daughter, moved closer and kissed her forehead. Chioma froze and looked at her mom, surprised at the unusual display of affection. Her mother who understood her daughter's feelings smiled at her and walked to the kitchen to prepare lunch for the family.

Chioma was still reading her storybook when her phone started ringing. She stood up and went to the sitting room to pick the phone she kept on the centre table in the sitting room. She chuckled when she saw who was calling her.

'Hi, Donald, I was wondering why you hadn't called today, knowing fully well that you never miss your calling time,' Chioma said on the phone excitedly.

Shortly after Chioma was discharged from the hospital, the N. Y. S. C (Nigeria Youth Service Corps) mobilised students from all the Nigerian higher institutions who were qualified to serve their fatherland. The National Youth Service Corps (N.Y.S.C) was a program set up by the Nigerian Government during the military regime to involve Nigerian graduates in nation building and the development of the country. Donald and Chioma were among the Nigerian students mobilised but because Chioma was still recovering, the doctors advised her to defer her National clarion call.

Donald was posted to Lagos for his one year service to the fatherland. Before Donald was posted to Lagos to serve, he usually visited Chioma twice a week at her family's house in Anambra State. Chioma's family welcomed Donald in their house because they saw him as a good friend who stood by their daughter's side throughout her darkest period. What led to him sleeping in Chioma's family house was as a result of what happened one certain day he visited Chioma to find out how she was faring.

That day it started raining heavily when Donald was about to go. Chioma's parents could not allow him to travel back to his State under that heavy rainfall, so they told Chioma's brother to prepare one of the guest rooms for him. Ever since then, he started sleeping in Chioma's family house whenever he felt he could not go back to his state the same day he visited. The last time he visited, he slept over in her house because he knew that once he went for service, he would not come back till the service year ended.

Donald occasionally cooked lunch or dinner for the family whenever he was around. The first day he attempted helping Chioma's mother in the kitchen, everybody in the house was surprised and attempted to stop him but he insisted. In Chioma's house, cooking was the ladies responsibility unlike in Donald's house where cooking was for any available person — both the males and the females. However, Chioma and her immediate family members had already seen Donald as part of the family.

Donald was doing all within his power to win Chioma's trust again. He did not know when he fell deeply in love with her. Conceivably, it was after he found out the wicked thing that John did to her. It was true that he also broke her heart by abandoning her after he slept with her. He had suddenly started feeling guilty after four months of dumping her. Soon, he lost appetite for other girls and realised he had deeply wronged her. His taste for friendships also changed. He started withdrawing from his crazy friends. It was then that he met Paul, a devoted Christian young man. It was Paul who advised him to plead for Chioma's forgiveness. Donald realised the gravity of what he did and started striving for her forgiveness.

'I am sorry, Chibaby, I have not had time to call because we were mandated to leave the NYSC orientation camp because of the outbreak of the COVID-19 Pandemic. We were given transportation fares to go back to our various houses. I called you as soon as I alighted from the car that brought me back from Lagos to Enugu State,' Donald patiently explained to Chioma on the phone.

Because of the nationwide outbreak of the coronial virus, the Nigerian government had declared a state of emergency in all the thirty-six states in Nigeria. People were mandated to stay in their houses, social gatherings were outlawed, and interstate travels were also banned in order to curtail the outbreak of the virus.

Chioma smiled as if Donald was watching her. She told him that she knew about it because she had listened to the morning news. She also explained to him that she called his phone but it was not reachable which made her worried.

*****　　*****　　*****

The Nigerian government with other governments of the world fought the COVID-19 pandemic with the whole of their strength. Unfortunately, a large number of people worldwide still lost their lives to the COVID-19 Pandemic. Donald and other Nigeria graduates who were mobilized to serve their fatherland stayed back in their houses, although the government still paid their monthly allowances. Because of this, Donald and the rest of those in his set were referred to as 'Corona virus Corpers' because they stayed in their houses during that period, which had never, happened since the inception of the NYSC.

Donald did not stop calling Chioma. They spoke on the phone almost every day. Donald was not happy that he could not travel to visit Chioma because of the interstate travel ban that was mandated as a result of the Covid outbreak.

As soon as interstate travel was approved, the first journey Donald embarked on was to Chioma's state. Both were excited to see each other and their exuberance was visible. Donald had already made up his mind to sleep in Chioma's family house before he embarked on the journey. However, Chioma did not go close to Donald's room. All their discussions took place in the sitting room where others could see them.

The time soon came for Donald to leave. Chioma sat down on one of the sofas in the sitting room. She was worried that Donald might not be able to find a bus to take him back to Enugu State. Donald who was in his room in Chioma's family house was intentionally delaying himself. He wanted to leave the house later. Thus, after preparing breakfast for the family, he went to his room and slept off. Chioma's parents did not bother waking him up even though they knew he was to travel back to his state that morning. Chioma's dad had gone to work, her mom to the shop, and her brother had gone to school. However, they were not afraid of leaving Chioma with Donald alone in the house because they trusted him.

When it was about 11 am, Chioma could not take it again. She went straight to Donald's room and pushed the door open. She was shocked to see Donald focused on his phone on the bed. It was the first time she would enter Donald's room when he was around. Donald smiled as if he knew she would come to check up on him. She froze upon seeing the subtle smile on his face. She pretended to be angry with him.

'Donald, you are here focused on your phone as if you are not travelling again today. Don't even dream of staying back because you know you are required to report at your P. P. A. (Place of Primary Assignment) in the next two days. If you fail to do so, you will not be paid your monthly salary or you may even have an extended service year,' she angrily told him.

Donald, who seemed not to care, lazily stood up from the bed and started folding a few of his clothes on the bed inside his school bag. She was not sure if she wanted him to go because she had already developed deep feelings for him but she carefully concealed her emotions from him. She stood there looking at him while he quietly packed his things. She wanted to cry out to stop him from parking but she could not do that. All she did was stand and admire him.

When Donald finished, he walked to her and gently made her sit on the bed. She did not fight Donald and sat on the bed facing him. Deep in her heart, she wanted Donald to hug her but she did not dare make the first move.

It was as if Donald understood Chioma's thoughts. He knelt in front of her and put his head on her lap. She was afraid to put her hands on his back but she did not push him away. Donald remained like that for some minutes before raising his head. His face went close to her face. She did not resist him. She admired his handsome face. Before she knew what was happening, he had already pressed his seductive lips on hers. She did not stop him. Rather, she closed her eyes and actively responded to his kiss.

Donald kissed her passionately as if his life depended on it. The kissing lasted for a while before he removed his lips from hers. Chioma was soon aroused because of the long kiss. After what John did to her, she had not allowed any guy to come close to her. Donald was the first person she allowed to come close to her since the incident.

'Let's not go beyond this until the time is right,' Donald told her, barely able to breathe the words out.

Chioma glimmered, wondering what he meant by 'when the time was right'. Donald who was still kneeling before her brought out an engagement ring from his trousers' pocket.

'Bestie, please be my wife and give me the privilege of being your husband. I promise to love you forever,' Donald said as he waited with bated breath for her response. He feared she would refuse him.

Chioma froze as she stared at him in shock. Tears ran down her eyes. She hastily wiped her eyes with the back of her palm.

'Donald, it's true I have deeply fallen in love with you and I know you love me too. But that is not enough reason for me to make this great commitment to you. Go and finish your service first. You can come back and propose to me after I am done with my own one year service. That's only if you will still be interested in me,' she said, carefully watching for his response.

Donald could not stop his tears again. 'What if another man takes you before you finish your service?' Donald asked her, amidst his tears.

Chioma did not respond immediately. She stood up from the bed walked to the door. When she got to the door, she stopped and turned. She said to him, 'Donald, if you come back after my NYSC and find out that I have married another man, then know that it is not God's will for us to be together.' She left the room, ignoring Donald who was

still kneeling.

TEN

'Good afternoon baby,' Chioma greeted her husband who was standing at the door and threw herself at him. He hugged her tightly. It took them some minutes before they left themselves.

'I was so worried about you. I called your number but you did not answer. I thought you were sleeping and I did not want to disturb you, so I did not call again. When I returned and did not see you, I went downstairs and asked the gateman to tell me where you were, but he told me that you had left since morning and did not tell him where you were going. I was about dialling your number before I heard your car horn outside the gate,' Chioma's husband said worriedly. He held her and gave her a punishing kiss for making him worry about her. Chioma, laughing, managed to push him away and both of them walked into the house.

The house was glamorous both on the inside and outside. The painting of the house was golden. Everything inside the house was made with gold. The walls were painted gold. Anybody who saw the magnificent building would know that the owners of the house were indeed wealthy.

'Darling, I'm sorry for making you scared. I'm perfectly fine. I promise not to frighten you again,' Chioma sincerely apologised to her husband.

She wanted to explain to her husband where she went but he insisted that she would not explain. Instead, he told her to eat first before explaining. He had noticed that his wife did not eat the breakfast he made for her before he left. He was not able to force her to eat before leaving in the morning because he left on time. Often, her husband prepared breakfast before leaving for work, mostly because he had overworked her most nights with all-night lovemaking. Chioma did not find any word to refute him as she was already used to his overly caring attitude. Sometimes, she felt choked up with his love but she still enjoyed the maximum love and attention he gave her.

She went to their room and took her bath, changing over to her casual wear. She usually took ample time to bathe. Before she finished, her husband had already set jollof rice and chicken on the dinner table for her. Already hungry, she did not waste time eating the food once she got to the table. When she finished, he served her fruit juice.

'Baby, thank you for the food,' Chioma instantly thanked her husband when she finished eating.

'Honey, you can now tell me where you went to. I'm listening,' he told her in a low, sexy voice.

She smiled and said, 'Baby, I met John today when I went to the hospital.'

The water Donald was drinking almost choked him when he heard John's name.

'Honey, John who almost killed you? Did he hurt you? What happened?' Donald asked, rambling with a trembling voice.

'Baby, calm down, he dared not touch me. A young man and a lady in her late thirties approached me when I was about to open my car door to drive out of the hospital. I was able to recognize the young man when he removed the sunglass he was wearing. Resentment and bitterness from nowhere filled my heart immediately. I wanted to ignore them, enter my car and drive out but the lady with him stopped me from opening my car door with her pleading eyes. John finally spoke and told me that we needed to find a place to sit and talk. Once bitten twice shy. I coarsely declined his request. In my heart, I pitied the lady he was with. I saw her as his potential victim.

'It was as if John had accessed my mind and knew what I was thinking. He told me that the lady was not his victim but his wife. The lady gave me a reassuring smile which made me believe John though I still had doubts and fears in my heart. The lady pleaded with me to follow them to the hospital lounge so we could sit and talk. I reluctantly agreed to follow them knowing that the hospital was safe and would not easily be harmed.' Chioma stopped talking. She fetched another glass of juice to drink. Her husband was patiently waiting for her to finish her encounter with John.

Chioma inhaled and exhaled hardly before she continued talking.

'At the hospital lounge, he ordered three bottles of soft drinks for us but I refused to take anything. The lady was the first person who spoke. She narrated how she left her husband John with her kids a year ago to go live with her ex-boyfriend when she found out that her husband was having extramarital affairs. It was quite unfortunate that her ex-boyfriend started coming around when her husband was misbehaving. She started going on dates with her ex-boyfriend with the mindset of finding happiness and comfort but unknowingly to her, she was entering the trap of her ex who was determined to ruin her marriage. She had already made up her mind to divorce her husband and marry her ex-boyfriend before his intention for revenge became exposed.

'Her ex-boyfriend had always felt that she turned down his marriage proposal and had married John because

John was wealthier than him. The two later coincidentally met at a shopping mall after many years they lost contact. He pretended that he still loved her and desired her whereas he was filled with bitterness. He told her that he was not able to find love again after she left him. Beyond every doubt, he proved to her that he still loved her. He convinced her to leave her husband and stay with him since her husband had become imperfect for her. She refused initially but when her husband's attitude became unbearable for her, she took a few of her clothes and left to her ex-boyfriend's house.

'She was pleased to see that her ex-boyfriend had become more established. Her husband John tried all he could to plead with her and bring her back home but she refused. The day she left her ex's house and went back to her husband's house was the day she came back and gave her ex-boyfriend a pregnancy report she got from the hospital. Despite her mixed feelings, she was happy that, at least, the pregnancy for would help her to make a quick decision on finally divorcing her husband and getting married to her first love.

'When she handed the pregnancy result to her ex-boyfriend, he smiled viciously and then told her that he had succeeded on his mission. She was still trying to understand what he meant but his next action explained vividly to her what he was talking about. He jumped on her like an angry mad man and beat her blue-black. He left her in the pool of her blood after raping her severally. At midnight, when she finally woke up, she noticed that nobody was in the house except her. She was experiencing excruciating pains all over her body but managed to carry her handbag and ran out of the house by that time of the night. She was lucky that her ex did not lock her inside the house and she was able to find a taxi that took her to her husband's house.'

Chioma took a deep breath again and continued. 'When she reached her husband's house, she alighted from the taxi and used the last strength in her to walk to the gate and typed in the house secret code. When the gate opened, she walked in and slumped. She said that John who had been restless throughout that day without knowing the cause rushed to the gate immediately he saw her entering the gate from the security camera in his room. He quickly drove her to their family hospital where she was admitted for three days before she fully recovered. Her pregnancy was also terminated because it endangered her life.

John did not waste time to forgive his wife and accepted her back because he deciphered it was karma playing out. Ever since then, John had turned out to be the most perfect husband to his wife and his wife also purposed in her heart not to ruin her marriage again with her selfishness.' Chioma smiled at her husband and continued. 'The couple apologized to me and I sincerely forgave John because I knew it is God who perfects the imperfections of men.'

Donald looked at his wife with great admiration. Oblivious to the way her husband was looking at her, Chioma eagerly disclosed to him her reason for going to the hospital. Meanwhile, lost in thought, Donald did not say a word to her. He thanked God in his heart that he had married Chioma. He felt his life would have been miserable if she had refused to marry him. He did not waste time to propose to her after she finished her one year service. After two months of courtship, they did their traditional marriage at Anambra State, and court wedding at Lagos State. Donald's parents gave him a Villa at Banana Island, Lagos, as a wedding gift. Banana Island was in the heart of Lagos. It was a few wealthy people could afford to live there. It was considered to be the most expensive place to live in Lagos. The Villa, Donald's parents gifted him was among the five best Villas at the Banana Island.

'Baby, as soon as you left for the embassy to get our travelling documents ready, I started feeling sick. I didn't want to disturb you so I decided against calling you. I went straight to the nearby hospital to get some medication. But when I got there, the doctor ran some tests on me and told me that I was one month pregnant,' Chioma patiently let out.

Donald's joy knew no bounds. He jumped up from the seat where he was and ran to Chioma. He hugged her tightly, thanking her repeatedly for saying yes to him. He also thanked God for making him a father sooner than he anticipated, as their marriage was only two months old. He vowed to her that he would be the best husband to her and a good father to their child.

They would not just be leaving Lagos, but Nigeria entirely before the end of the month. Meanwhile, Chioma had already secured admission in Harvard University, United States, to continue with her studies. Donald completed his Masters' Program with the scholarship he obtained from the University of Nigeria, Nsukka. He currently worked in one of the biggest firms in Lagos. When he was processing his travel papers, the firm he worked with wrote a letter of transfer which was sent to their headquarter branch in the United States. They did not want to lose such a sharp brain to others. He also intended to further his studies over there. Chioma who had not used the scholarship given to her in the University of Nigeria, Nsukka, as the best graduating student of the year to study in any university of her choice, would use the scholarship to further her studies at Harvard University.

Donald was extremely delighted and did not mind that they were outside their room. He pressed his hungry lips against hers and kissed her passionately. Chioma gasped for air before he left her mouth. Then, he passionately made love to her.

Printed in Great Britain
by Amazon

22184259R00101